THE GUILDSMAN

A Vow of Duty

By Ryan Darkfield

Acknowledgements

Roger Victor Richards
Glyn, Claire and Lucas Richards
Sarah Baugh
Chris and Donna Edwards
Warren McCabe
Ash Fowkes
Emily Bates
Ellie Lauren Edwards
Les Richards
Bentley

and
Gaynor Richards

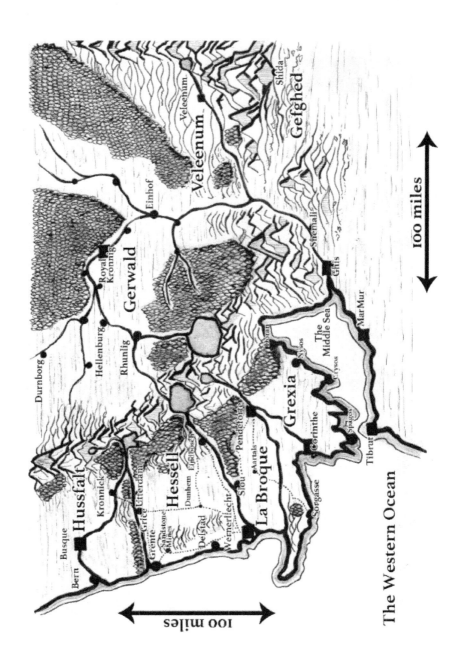

The Western Ocean

100 miles

Prologue

Dirk trembled with fear.

He'd never seen his father like this.

The man was shaking, flustered.

He was dashing around the room, picking up their things and stuffing them inside a large wooden chest.

"Help me," he ordered, his voice laden with fear. "We need to leave this place as soon as possible!"

Dirk's night had been a quiet one until now, and he had been sitting out on the balcony watching the Elves dancing in the streets below. It was midsummer and they were celebrating the birthday of their prophet, the Goddess, Sheenah.

It looked fun and Dirk would have snuck down and joined them if his father's last words to him hadn't been so stern or his tone so insistent.

"Don't leave the room while I'm gone," he'd told him. "And answer the door to no one but me."

Dirk had done as he was told and had not left the room.

It was lonely being by himself.

It was times like these when he wished he'd had a brother. His father had promised him one back when his mother was alive, but her death had put paid to that.

Instead of remarrying, Minas had thrown himself into his work, taking Dirk with him as he carted his wares from town to town. In the five years since his mother had died, he'd lost count of all the places they had been. Starting in Hellenburg, they'd worked their way south through Gerwald and had crossed the border into the colonies, visiting Shida, Shemali, and now finally, Ghis.

Dirk disliked the southern lands.

He found the weather too hot and dry.

His fair skin burned easily in the sun, and the sand and dust irritated his eyes. He longed for the day they would return home, to a place where the skies were grey, where grass covered meadows, and forests lined the lakes.

His father had told him it would happen one day.

"As soon as I have the coin, we'll return," he'd said.

But Dirk doubted it would ever happen.

Even at his young age he had the nous to realise that little money could be made from the selling of trinkets and ornaments, and that sooner or later Minas would have to sell his cart and find work in the city.

The two months they'd spent in Ghis had all but convinced him of this, as their lack of funds had seen them move lodgings three times already, with each new place being worse than the last.

At times his father had appeared desperate and inconsolable, but despite his dour mood, he'd never raised his voice in anger.

Until now...

"What are you doing?" Minas roared. "You don't need that. Leave it behind!"

"But it's *Beni*, father," Dirk replied, holding up his wooden horse.

His father snatched it from his hand and threw it across the room.

"It's just a toy," he snapped.

Dirk was shocked.

His Mother had given it to him for his seventh birthday. It had been the last thing she'd given him before she'd died...

But now it was 'just a toy'.

A worthless piece of wood...

Dirk sobbed.

"Stop crying," his father ordered. "I'll buy you another when we get to Hellenburg."

"We're going home?" Dirk exclaimed.

His spirits were suddenly lifted.

"Yes," Minas replied. "And the sooner you pack, the sooner we'll leave."

Dirk quickly gathered his clothes and threw them inside his carry case. He then flipped the lid and secured the latch.

"I'm ready," he said.

His father picked up the wooden chest and went to the door.

Dirk followed behind, dragging his case across the floorboards.

"Wait," his father said. "I'll need to check it's clear."

He turned the latch and held the door ajar then peered down the corridor.

"It's safe," he whispered. "Let's go."

Dirk followed him out of the room and then down the staircase at the end of the hall. At the bottom they turned right, then quickly made their way toward the back door.

"Father," Dirk called, as he struggled to keep up. "Don't we need to tell Jurgash we're leaving?"

He was the Inn's owner, a kindly man with a warm smile. He'd always been nice to Dirk, so he wanted to say goodbye.

"There's no time," his father replied.

"But we haven't paid..."

"It doesn't matter."

Minas opened the outside door, which led to the small courtyard at the rear over the tavern. To their right was a large awning that covered the stables. Several horses were inside.

"Untie Bess and bring her out," Minas said.

Dirk nodded and went over to the light brown mare, patting her lightly on the cheek as he unravelled her bridle.

"We're going home, girl," he whispered. "Isn't that good?"

The horse whinnied in response.

Dirk took Bess by the bit and brought her into the centre of the yard, where Minas connected her to the harness.

While he was doing this, Dirk glanced at the trailer.

It appeared to be fully laden, creaking under the weight.

He wondered what was beneath the canvass.

Whatever it was, it was heavy.

"What's in the cart?" Dirk asked.

"Coin," his father replied, as he lifted the tug over Bess' head. "Lots of it. Enough to buy us a house."

6

Dirk smiled.

"Does that mean no more travelling?"

"No more travelling," his father replied.

Dirk got up onto the seat then watched his father run across the yard to the gate. After swinging it open, he rushed back and climbed up onto the driver's bench then flicked the reins across Bess' back.

She snorted and trotted forward, and he guided her out onto the street. They turned towards the Eastern Gate and as they passed through it, Dirk saw the first light of dawn appearing over the Shemali Hills.

His heart was immediately filled with hope. Today would mark a new start, a chance to put the hardship of the last five years behind them.

He nuzzled his father's shoulder as Bess dragged them out onto the Colony Road, which would take them north to Gerwald.

And home.

* * *

After several hours of riding, they passed through the Silent Valley, a canyon that lay close to the Imperial border.

It was deathly quiet, all sound drowned out by the high cliffs of dirt that stood on either side, and Dirk could hear nothing but the clopping of hooves and the dull creaking of the cart's wheels.

It was creepy here, and he didn't like it.

"How long will it take us to get home?" he asked.

"Five nights, give or take," his father replied.

"Will we stop at any Inns on the way?" Dirk asked.

"We'll stay at the finest Inns, son," Minas replied. "And we'll eat like kings every night."

"What if I don't want to stop at the Inns?" Dirk said.

"Then we'll camp beneath the stars," his father replied.

His mood had improved since leaving Ghis. He seemed

less anxious now, much calmer.

"How about we stop by the river later," he asked, "catch some eels for supper?"

"I'd like that," Dirk replied. "It'll be like that time we all went fishing in the lake."

Minas smiled and turned his head to the front.

He suddenly seemed sad.

"I'm sorry about your horse, son," he said. "I didn't mean to break it."

"It's ok father," Dirk replied. "It was just a toy."

"I know," his father said. "But it was special to you."

"Then why did you do it?" Dirk asked.

"We were in a rush," he replied. "We needed to leave."

"Why?" he asked.

His father had yet to explain to him why they had been in such a hurry.

Minas sighed and looked to the front.

"I'll tell you one day," he replied. "When you're older."

Dirk was confused.

"Why not now?" he asked.

But his father wouldn't answer.

Dirk sat leant back in his seat and folded his arms.

"Don't be like that," his father said. "We'll soon be home and none of this will matter."

Before he could reply, the silence of the valley was shattered by a sickening howl.

Dirk stood up on the bench and turned toward the sound.

Five riders were coming up the road from the south.

They were driving their horses hard.

"What is it?" his father asked.

"Men," Dirk replied. "Behind us."

Minas looked over his shoulder and gasped.

"V'Loire," he cried. "Sit down and hold on!"

Dirk jumped down and took hold of the dashboard as his father lashed the reins over Bess' back. The mare upped her pace from a canter to a gallop, and the cart shuddered as its wheels turned faster over the dusty pebble-flecked road.

Dirk glanced back over his shoulder.

The riders were closing in.

As they drew nearer, he noticed the pointed tips of their ears poking out from beneath their hoods.

They weren't men at all.

They were Elves.

"They're getting closer!" he yelled.

His father screamed at Bess to go faster.

The mare found an extra burst of pace, and the cart began to pull clear ...

But then suddenly it jolted and began to slow.

Dirk looked down and saw one of its wheels spinning away into the dirt.

The bandits cheered and one of them spurred his horse alongside the cart.

Dirk noticed that he was holding a sword.

He took a swipe it at Minas, who ducked low to avoid being struck. The sudden movement caused him to pull down on the reins and Bess veered to the right, dragging the trailer across the road. As its weight shifted over the missing wheel, the reaches split, and with a mighty crash, the cart crumpled into the ground.

The impact threw Dirk from his seat, and he was flung many yards through the air. He landed hard, rolling several yards before coming to a stop.

He lifted his head from the dusty ground, and in daze saw the five Elven riders surrounding the stricken cart.

Their leader, a tall man with greying hair and a patch covering his right eye, climbed down from his saddle and approached the wreckage of the driver's block, where he seized Dirk's father by the collar and lifted him from the debris.

The Elf dragged him to the rear of the trailer and pointed to the chests that had been loaded inside. Minas dropped to his knees and crossed his hands, pleading for his life. Dirk watched in horror as the Elf drew the dagger from his belt and coolly ran the blade across his father's throat.

As his body crumbled to the ground, Dirk's heart crumbled in his chest.

For a split second, time stood still.

With a deft flick of his wrist, the man had taken everything from him...

He looked up his father's one-eyed killer, and from the remnants of his broken heart a burning fire raged.

He was angry, furious.

He wanted to kill the man where he stood.

At once he leapt to his feet and ran towards the man holding the knife.

His comrades yelling a warning as Dirk drew closer, and the Elf spun round with his arm outstretched. The blow caught him on the side of his head, and he tumbled to the ground.

He felt dizzy and tasted dirt in his mouth.

He glanced up and saw that the man was laughing.

Dirk howled in rage, but as he got up off the floor the man kicked him in the stomach. The blow winded him and he curled up into a ball, gasping.

"Stop toying with him," one of his friends said. "Kill him and be done with it."

"No," another one retorted. "We don't kill children. It's against Sheenah's will."

"Fine," he said. "We'll leave him here."

"But he's a witness," the first Elf replied.

His father's killer looked around at the desolate landscape.

"The desert leaves no witnesses," he smirked.

The first Elf chuckled and climbed down from his horse then Dirk watched from the ground as the bandits took the sacks of coin from the trailer's ruin and loaded them onto the backs of their horses.

Another one approached the front of cart, where Bess lay snorting amongst the debris. The man drew his sabre and plunged it into her side.

She yelped then fell silent.

Dirk picked himself up and cursed them under his breath as they returned to their horses and climbed up onto their saddles. With a yell of triumph, they galloped away down the road, leaving nothing behind but a cloud of dust.

When silence returned to the valley, Dirk stumbled over to his father's body and knelt down by his side, tears welling in his eyes.

Parts of the mangled cart were littered on the earth around him, as smashed and broken as his world.

He lifted his father's hand and held it in his own.

Why had this happened, he asked himself?

His father was a good man...

He didn't deserve this...

Why?

He sobbed into his hands and howled at the sky.

Then he bent over on his haunches, palmed his hands, and prayed to V'Loire for guidance.

His plea was answered by the sound of thundering hooves beyond the ridge.

Were they coming back, he thought?

Had they changed their mind and decided to kill him?

If so, he'd be ready this time.

Reaching out, he picked up a long shaft of wood that had splintered from the cart. Holding it in his hand like a sword, he turned to face the riders.

Three figures appeared on the ridge.

All of them were dressed in dark grey tunics and wore long swords at their sides.

They started coming down the hill towards him.

Dirk raised his stick in the air.

He wasn't afraid.

He was angry.

He wanted to fight.

He wanted to kill the men who had murdered his father.

As the riders drew nearer, he noticed the polished iron seals that had been stitched into the lapels of their tunics.

They were Guildsmen: Guardians of the Law and Protectors of Justice.

They brought their horses to a halt and their leader, an older man with a long moustache, climbed down from his saddle.

"Don't be afraid lad," he said. "We won't harm you."

Dirk stepped back and raised his stick.

The man stood still and lifted his hands.

"We're here to help," he said. "We want to know who did this."

"Elves," Dirk shouted.

"Which way did they go?" asked one of the man's comrades. "Tell us, so we can find them."

"I don't know," Dirk yelled.

"He's lying," the man replied.

The older Guildsman growled.

"Silence," he barked. "Can't you see what's happened here?"

"I can," the other man grumbled as he dismounted, "but our time would be better spent finding their tracks, rather than listening to the sobs of a bawling child."

He pointed at Dirk.

Dirk saw red.

He charged forward, lifting the point of his stick high in the air. The younger man was taken by surprise, barely having time to raise his arms as Dirk began whipping his chest and shoulders.

"Stop it," the man barked, "or I'll give you a hiding."

The third man, who has remained in his saddle throughout, started laughing.

"I think he's beat you to it," he chuckled.

"Enough," the older man roared.

He stepped forward and snatched the stick from Dirk's hands.

Dirk spun round and threw a punch at his stomach. The man responded by slapping him across the face.

It wasn't a hard blow, but enough to knock Dirk off his feet. Undaunted, he picked himself up, but the man took him by the scruff of the neck and held him down on his haunches.

"I know you're hurting lad," he rasped. "But fighting us won't help."

Dirk hissed at him.

"Let's just leave him," the younger man said. "He's of no use to us."

The older man turned round and struck him in the face.

"Are you out of your mind?" he said. "You swore to protect the innocent! We all did."

The younger man's eyes drifted to floor.

He looked ashamed, embarrassed.

"Fine," the third man said. "But what will we do with him?"

The older man turned round.

He looked Dirk in the eye.

"Do you want vengeance on the men who did this?" he asked.

Dirk glanced at the body of his father and nodded.

"Then come with us."

CHAPTER 1

Dirk woke with a start.

He'd been dreaming again.

It was the same dream he'd had each night for the past six years.

He sat up in his bunk and began rubbing his eyes. The air in the dormitory was cold, but he was comforted at the sight of his breath steaming in front of his face. It served to remind him where he was, the Guildschool in Royal Kronnig, far removed from the setting of his nightmare...

He heard groaning from the other recruits who were waking up around him. He looked across to their bunks and saw them tossing and turning in their beds.

"Bad dream?" Coen asked.

Dirk looked over to the adjacent bed and saw his friend sweeping the tousled blonde locks from his eyes.

Dirk nodded.

"The same one?" the lad asked, swinging his legs over the side of the bunk.

Dirk didn't answer.

Though his nightmares were no secret to the other recruits, he'd never discussed their content.

They were his burden to bear, and his alone.

A low groaning from his right heralded the awakening of Ing.

"I wish I could sally off into a dream world..." he grumbled.

Dirk glanced over to the opposite bunk and saw the Rhunligger burying his mottled face into his pillow.

"Anything to escape the drudgery of this place..."

Coen chuckled.

"It's *Passing Out* day and this one's still moaning!" he remarked.

"Unlike you, I'm not here for the fun of it," Ing replied.

The second part was true.

Ing was here under duress.

After his father, the Count of Rhunlig, had been charged with Treason and had killed himself to avoid the shame of execution, the Crown had ordered his son to pay penance by offering his services to the Guild.

Coen shrugged.

"There's no pleasing some people," he remarked.

"What's to be pleased about?" Ing snorted. "After today, the Guild owns us for twenty-five years."

"...Which you'll serve with honour and pride," Coen finished.

Of all the recruits, Coen was the most dutiful. Part of this had been down to his upbringing. Both of his parents had served the Guild, and he was keen to follow in their footsteps.

Forever diligent and mindful of the rules, he carried himself proudly wherever he went, and inspired his fellow recruits with encouraging words. It was something that made him very unpopular with the other recruits, who regarded him a sycophant.

"I'd better serve the cause from my bed," Ing replied, his voice muffled beneath the pillow.

Dirk laughed.

Bunked between Coen's optimism and Ing's pessimism, he had the worst of both worlds.

The morning bugle sounded in the yard outside and a collective murmur swept across the bunks. Though it was their final day at the Guild School, and thus a reason for celebration, lads of eighteen rarely enjoyed being summoned from their beds, and today was no exception.

Dirk swung his legs over the side of his bunk and dropped

to the floor. He then went to the end of his bed and pulled his uniform out of the chest.

After putting on his slacks, he threaded his arms into the sleeves of his dark grey tunic and fixed the garment tightly across his chest. He then slid his feet inside his knee-high boots and made his way over to the basin in the corner of the room, where he washed and shaved with the other recruits, before combing back his hair and tying it into a neat bun at the base of his neck.

He stepped back and looked at himself in the mirror.

He'd aged much in the time he'd been here. Gone were the skinny arms and short stature that had defined him as a child; in their place stood the strong body and chiselled features of a handsome young man. He wondered whether his father would recognise him if he saw him now? Would he believe the man now standing before him had once been the weak and fretful child he'd raised?

He sighed then glanced out of the window.

Through the gloom of the early autumnal morning, he saw servants working in the courtyard, hanging drab bunting from the stage that had been erected for the *Passing Out* ceremony.

At once, he was struck by the enormity of it all.

The school had been his life for such a long time.

From tomorrow, it would all change.

The dormitory door opened and the imposing form of their Master of Arms, Major Patz, entered the room. He was tall, broad, and younger than the other officers. The reason for this hung limply from his right shoulder: an empty sleeve that was missing an arm. It was an injury that had ended his service prematurely, but rather than riding off into the sunset to spend his generous pension, he'd opted to join the school and continue his work, training the next generation of Guildsmen.

"Passing Out time, recruits," he yelled with his booming regimental voice. "Time for you to take your vows and cross the threshold into manhood."

Dirk brushed down his tunic and straightened the lace of

his epaulettes. He then followed the crush of recruits to the door, where they formed up into line.

"Here we go," Coen said, as the Major led them out. "It's all upwards from here!"

"Roll on retirement..." Ing groaned.

* * *

Dirk followed the line outside as a light rain fell down from the grey skies overhead. The Major stopped at the foot of the stage, and ordered the recruits to form up into five rows of eight.

Once they were in position, he called them to attention and the men responded by straightening their backs and stamping down on the floor with the heels of their boots.

The door to the main hall then opened and out came Guildmaster Patrick, the School's Head, accompanied by a servant who was carrying a small chest striped with golden bands.

Respected and revered by every student and mentor alike, the Guildmaster was a living legend among the *Fraternity of Finders*. Silver haired and aged, he'd seen through it all during his seventy years' service; from the signing of the *Finders Covenant*, which had granted the Guild its licence to practice in Gerwald, to the adoption of the more recent *Westren Concordant*, which allowed its members the freedom to serve in the neighbouring states of Hussfalt, Hessell, La Broque and Grexia.

He climbed up onto the stage then stepped forward to address them, his face a picture of pride.

"Recruits," he said, in his dulcet Rhundian brogue, "Today is a very special day for each and every one of you..."

Dirk glanced at Coen; whose broad smile beamed through the morning gloom.

"...It is the day you finally earn your seal and earn your place among this Order."

He paused and wiped the pooling raindrops from his long eyebrows.

"But before you earn the *Iron Seal*," he continued, "You must first take your *Vows of Service.*"

Dirk looked to his left and saw Ing stifling a yawn.

The Guildmaster stepped forward and called for the *Valedictorian*, the recruit who'd graduated with the highest honours.

It came as no surprise that this was Coen, and the blonde-haired starlet marched forward and climbed the stairs of the stage, where he stood before the Guildmaster and bowed.

The wizened old man nodded in return then gestured for the lad to kneel before him.

"Now," the Guildmaster said. "Your Vow of Duty."

Coen took a deep breath then started reciting the words.

"I, Coen Brendt, do solemnly swear to uphold the Vow of Duty. I promise to follow the orders of my superiors; to never question their motives, and to always act in accordance with their will."

The old man nodded

"And now the Vow of Succour," he said.

Coen took another breath then began his second vow.

"I swear to uphold the Vow of Succour," the lad continued, "To protect the innocent from harm, and to never, by action nor omission, allow the innocent to be hurt or harmed by my deeds so long as I wear my seal."

The Guildmaster bobbed his head.

"And finally," he said, "the most important vow of all. The Vow of Honour."

Coen took a third breath.

"I do solemnly swear to uphold the Vow of Honour," he said. "To never dishonour the Guild by my actions or omissions; to conduct myself in a way befitting of a Guildsman at all times, and to never bring the Guilds of Finders into disrepute."

Once he'd finished speaking, he let out a deep sigh and allowed himself half a smile.

The Guildmaster gestured for him to stand then beckoned his servant forward.

"In recognition of the vows you have taken," the Guildmaster said, "I now present you with the Iron Seal."

He reached inside the chest with golden bands and took out one of the many metal brooches that had been placed inside, a breastpin fashioned into the shape of an all-seeing eye.

"Let this serve as a reminder of the vows you have taken this day," he said, as he pinned it to Coen's lapel.

"May you wear it with pride…" the Guildmaster said reverently. "…And do nothing to lessen its shine."

The lad then turned and saluted the other recruits by touching his seal with a closed fist. Dirk watched as he then made his way off stage and returned to his place among his comrades with a smug look on his face.

"Someone looks happy," Ing chuckled, under his breath.

The Guildmaster stepped to the front of the stage.

"And now the next recruit," he declared. "Dirk Vanslow."

* * *

The ceremony continued throughout the morning, and the recruits stood to attention throughout. Many grown men would have wilted from the process, but Dirk and his classmates stood firm, their bodies primed for the task by many years of physical training.

This was something the school took seriously, and all recruits, regardless of their size, strength, or stature, were required to participate in a daily morning run around the *Nordfeld*, the Capital's largest park. This was followed by an hour of wrestling, then two hours of swordsmanship in the early afternoon.

After lunch, the rest of the day would be spent learning more classical subjects, such as History, Theology and *Prutch*; the idea being that Guildsmen should be thinkers as well as fighters.

Once the final recruit had taken his vows and had saluted his colleagues, the Guildmaster called an end to the ceremony and congratulated the class of 1215 for their efforts. He then left the stage with his servant and returned inside.

Once he was out of sight, the Major came to the fore.

"Right men," he yelled. "Who's up for a drink to celebrate?"

A huge cheer went up from the yard.

"Finally," Ing declared. "Something to get excited about."

The officer gestured to a servant who was standing at the back of the yard, who nodded and swung open the gate.

With a loud roar the recruits stormed toward the exit.

"Remember who you are, and what you represent" Patz yelled behind them, "...Or you'll be losing those Seals as soon as you've earned them!"

Dirk followed the throng of graduates to the nearest bar on the square, a Tavern named the 'Emperor's Legs'. The owner, a stout man named Bartheld, was an ex-Guildsman and had pre-pared himself for *Passing Out* day by laying out several kegs of *Grott's Ale.* As soon as Ing saw the barrels lined up at the bar, he pushed his way to the front, where he poured himself a mug and necked it in one. He then started laughing and dancing on the tables like a man possessed. In the six years he'd known him, Dirk had never seen him look so happy.

After filling up his own glass, Dirk joined Coen at a table by the window.

"You're not drinking?" Dirk said.

"I need a clear head for tomorrow," the lad replied.

Dirk smirked.

"Why?" he asked.

"I've applied for the Guild Corps," he replied.

Dirk had heard of them. They were the wing of the Order that dealt with internal governance. Competition for places was fierce and admittance was granted only to those who passed a written examination.

"I'm sure you'll be fine," Dirk said.

"I hope so," Coen replied. "Joining the Corps is my dream."

"Why?" Dirk laughed. "You'd rather catch Guildsmen than criminals?"

Coen chuckled.

"I want to follow in my father's footsteps," he replied. "He was Deputy Commander before he retired. I'm hoping to go one better."

"Lofty ambitions," Dirk remarked.

"There's nothing wrong with setting goals for yourself," Coen chuckled. "What about you?"

"I'm applying to join the Guild in Ghis," he replied.

Coen looked shocked.

"Why there?" he asked.

"I like the heat," Dirk lied. "...And with the Separatists doing what they're doing, I'll never get bored."

"I'd never put myself in that kind of danger to avoid boredom," Coen replied, "but if that's your poison, good luck to you."

"You too," Dirk said, raising his glass.

He glanced around the room at the other recruits, who were now in full swing. A number of them, including Ing, were playing drinking games with the owner.

"I sure will miss this bunch," he lamented.

"Me too," Coen said. "I hope we keep in touch."

Dirk smiled.

"Our paths will cross again," he said. "I'm sure of it."

CHAPTER 2

The next morning, Dirk woke up a sore head.

It had been a long time since he'd last drank beer, and never anything as strong as *Grott's Ale*. He got out of bed, washed and dressed himself then made his way to the Recruiting Office, where he'd arranged to meet Major Patz regarding his posting.

He knocked on the door then waited until a voice inside called him in.

Dirk entered the room to find the officer sitting behind his desk with a cold compress pressed to his eyes. He'd made the mistake of joining the new recruits after dinner, and they'd rewarded him with a yard of Grott's on the proviso that he drank it in a single gulp.

The grizzled warrior had risen to the challenge, picking up the long glass in his free hand and downing the full thirty inches in one: a feat that had earned him the respect of his lieges... and a terrible hangover to boot.

"What do you want, Vanslow?" the Major asked, removing the towel from his forehead and folding it up on the desk.

"I've come to ask about my placement, Sir," Dirk replied.

The man gave him a curious look.

"What's wrong with it?" he replied. "Everything's in order. You're riding out to Hellenburg tomorrow."

"Yes," Dirk replied. "About that...."

He hesitated, trying to find the right words to say.

"Well, lad," Patz urged. "Spit it out."

"...I was wondering if I could be transferred to Ghis instead?"

Patz leant back on his chair.

"We've already discussed this," he said. "The colony is too dangerous a place for a new recruit."

He dipped the towel into a small bowl of water on the desk.

Dirk gritted his teeth.

He'd been expecting a battle.

"I want to go to Ghis, Sir," he replied.

Patz leant forward and studied his eyes.

"Why?" he asked.

"It's where my father was killed," Dirk began, as the image of the one-eyed Elf formed in his mind. "I want to help find the man responsible."

Patz cut his eyes at him.

"You know it's not our business to seek revenge," he snorted, picking up the compress and giving it a squeeze. "There's no place in the Guild for personal vendettas."

Dirk fumed but tried not to let it show.

"But Sir..." he began.

"...However," Patz interjected, "In your case I'm willing to make an exception."

Dirk was confused.

The Major dropped the towel on the desk then stood up and made his way to a bookcase on the far wall. There, he pulled a file from the shelf and laid it on the desk.

"I've read your papers," he said. "And I believe I know who killed your father."

"Who?" Dirk asked.

"An Elven Rebel named Araxys."

Finally, Dirk had a name to go with the face.

"He leads a faction called the *Swords of Sheenah*. They're one of many groups in Gefghed that are dedicated to the reestablishment of the Elven Triumvirate."

"....The cause to reunite the three Elven Kingdoms of Veleenum, Gefghed and Marmur," Dirk concluded.

Patz smiled.

"You know your History," he said. "That's good. But what

you won't learn from any book is that they're also the bastards that did this."

He raised the stump of his right arm up into the light.

"Before I took up the burden of teaching you runts how to fight," he began, "I served under Guildcaptain Haskin in Ghis. Back then, the separatists had only just begun to organise, and things were much safer... Or so we thought."

He sat down in his chair and his eyes drifted to the window.

"One day we were out on patrol in the Eastern Highlands, near Shemali," he began, "when a band of these pirates descended on us from the hills. They killed my brothers and captured me."

He let out a long sigh.

"Deciding they couldn't risk letting me go, they decided to execute me in the desert, by pinning me to the ground with my own sword."

His eyes drifted to the floor as he recalled the memory.

"Araxys did the deed himself... He took my *Hunter's Bite* and drove it through my arm into the dirt. The one-eyed cur smiled at me as he did it, happy with his work... There I lay in agony for a full day, thirsty, starving and bleeding... until I took the fateful decision to pull my flesh through the blade to free myself."

Patz sighed then looked up at him.

"I've heard you have nightmares," he said.

Dirk nodded.

"Well, I have them too," Patz said.

He placed a sheet of parchment onto the desk, picked up his quill and began scribing words onto it.

"I'm writing you a letter of recommendation that you'll hand in to the Guildsergeant at Ghis," he began. "His name is Bakker. He served under me, long ago. My words should be enough to convince him to allow you to join his team. They're a special unit who are looking for the *Swords*. If you want revenge, they're the ones who'll help you do it."

Dirk nodded then took the note.

"Don't thank me," Patz replied. "I'm doing you a disservice. I can promise you now that nothing good will come of this."

Dirk smiled wryly then slid the scroll beneath his belt.

He nodded then made his way to the door.

"One more thing, Dirk," the Major called.

He stopped and looked back.

"When you kill this dog," Patz said. "Send him my regards."

* * *

Dirk returned to his dormitory, where he found Coen and Ing waiting by his bunk.

"How did it go?" Coen asked.

Dirk responded with a smile.

Ing shook his head.

"You're an idiot," the Rhunligger replied. "The colonies are lawless places. You'll be lucky to survive the winter."

"Where are you posted?" Dirk replied.

"Durnborg, in the north" he replied. "It's quiet and the Inns open late."

"Sounds like a perfect fit for you," Dirk remarked.

"Better than the hell you're off to," Ing replied. "Have you not heard what the Rebels do to their captives?"

"Who says I'll be one?"

Ing puffed out his cheeks.

"You'd better not," he said, drawing Dirk in for a final embrace. "I've lots of plans for us when we retire."

"Does it involve copious amounts of alcohol?" Coen remarked.

Ing glared at him.

"It might," he said, before breaking into laughter.

After saying their final farewells, Dirk made his way to the stables, where a horse had been prepared for his journey.

"His name's Mott," the Farrier said as he approached its

stall.

"Mott?" Dirk asked.

He was a grey stallion with a silver mane.

"Aye," the stableman continued. "Named after his *mother*. He's a good steed, but he's got a mighty temper sometimes, so treat him with respect."

"How fast is he?" Dirk asked.

"It depends how much he likes you," the man replied with a grin.

Dirk climbed up into the saddle and patted the horse on the head. Then he dug his heels into the stallion's sides and geed him forward into the yard. The horse snorted aggressively, then trotted out with gusto.

"I've loaded the saddlebags with enough food for your journey," the farrier said. "And I've also put in a spare skein of water in case you run out. It's hot down south this time of year."

"I know," Dirk replied, with a smile.

He guided Mott through the gate and made his way left onto the *Imperialplatz*.

The main square of the Gerwaldian Capital was never quiet. Whatever time of day, whatever time of year, the plaza was always full of people milling to and fro: millers, merchants, Altarmen, shopkeepers, all going about their daily business. Most of them were unaware of the ugly guerrilla war that was being fought in their southern colony, preferring to keep their minds occupied with matters more pressing to them like earning money or paying bills...

It was no surprise the conflict had garnered little coverage in the *Imperial Post*, as the problems of the southern region were seen as a blight on the Empire's otherwise unblemished record, and it led to a degree of apathy towards the colony's plight.

Dirk could understand their indifference.

Having experienced the nightmares of his own personal tragedy, he'd come to appreciate the bliss of ignorance, and would gladly trade places with any one of them if he could.

He turned onto the *Sudenstrasse* and made his way toward

the fortified gate that guarded the bridge spanning the River Rhund. As he crossed over its dark blue waters, he glanced to its source in the West: the Grondils, a range of mountains, stretching from north to south, which separated the Empire from its Westren neighbours.

He wondered how different his life would have been if they didn't exist? For if nothing stood between Gerwald and the kingdoms of Westren, there would have been no reason for the Empire to conquer lands south of the border. Without the invasion, he thought, there would never have been a colony, and without a colony there would never have been a dispute, and without the dispute the separatists would have never had reason to rebel.

And if there were no rebels, his father would still be alive.

He shook his head and scolded himself for being so crass.

Geography was not to blame for his father's death.

The fault lay with Araxys and him alone.

Nothing could excuse what he'd done.

Not borders.

Not rivers.

Not mountains.

He held the thought in his mind as he joined the *Colony Road* to begin his long journey south.

* * *

It took four days to reach the Gefgheddi border. There, the road became nothing more than a dirt track as it snaked its way through the Silent Valley.

Dirk remembered the place from his dreams; the dry and arid landscape, the rocky ridges covered in dust and dirt, and above all... the deathly quiet.

He'd forgotten how warm it was too.

By midday, it had gotten so hot that he'd had to stop his horse and allow it to rest. As he drank from his skein, he looked around at the desolate landscape and at once realised that he was standing in the very place where his father had been murdered.

Two thousand days had passed since the crime and the gravelly floor betrayed no secrets as to what had happened. He'd never known what had become of his father's body, whether it'd been found, taken away and buried, or left to rot on the topsoil as carrion for the birds and animals.

The Guildsman who had found him had promised they'd sent men to recover the corpse, but no one had got in touch with him to tell him what had happened.

As far as Dirk knew, there had been no funeral and no song, two things required by the Faith to preserve a believer's soul.

He walked to and fro over the small stones that lined the ground, sweeping away the dust with his feet, looking for clues beneath the sand.

Suddenly, the heel of his boot brushed against something hard, and he dropped to his knees and began digging at the ground with his hands.

Buried just below the topsoil was a single golden Dram.

He wiped the coin on his sleeve and held it up to the light. Upon it, he saw the face of Count Lucas, the Governor of Gefghed. It was dated 1208.

Something told him it had belonged to his father and that it had been one of the coins that had spilled from his cart after it had crashed.

A tear welled in his eye as the memory of that fateful day returned to his mind.

Silently, he unsheathed the dagger from his waist and drew the blade along the flat of his hand. Placing the coin in his bloodied palm, he repeated the prayer he'd said for his father that day, before burying it in the sand and swearing to V'Loire he would bring vengeance upon his killer...

CHAPTER 3

It was early evening by the time the city of Ghis appeared on the Western horizon. Even though it was getting dark and he was several miles away, Dirk could see how much it had changed. Where before the spires of the Elven Temples had dominated the city's skyline, the central tower of the Citadel now loomed above them, it's plain stone façade brutally reflecting its darker purpose.

While he was in Kronnig, he'd learned that the castle had been built in response to the growing threat posed by the increasing number of Rebel factions.

Support for their cause was growing by the day, but their efforts to overthrow Imperial rule were hindered by their disunity, with many groups striving for different outcomes. Some wanted equal rights, others, equal pay for equal work. The more militant ones wanted Gerwald to leave the Kingdom entirely, or for the Elves to seize control and punish the colonists by forcing them into servitude.

A few factions went even further and were actively calling for the eradication of all humans from the southern lands. Those groups were the most fanatical and dangerous. The *Swords of Sheenah* were among them.

As he approached the Eastern gate, he came across a shanty that had been erected outside the city walls. Many people were living there, mostly Elves, who appeared dirty and poor. As he rode by, a group of small children approached his horse with their arms outstretched, begging for money and food. He reached into his purse and took out a handful of coins and tossed them into their air, the children swarming where they landed like pigeons around breadcrumbs.

The closer he came to the gate, the more impoverished the township became. He saw people living in huts made from discarded materials, with roofs made from broken cane that barely provided any shelter. Entire families wearing nothing but rags, sat outside them huddled around tiny stoves made from old helmets …

Unable to help, he turned away.

There was little he could do.

He was but a Guildsman.

Feeding the poor was a problem for the Governor.

A cadre of human guards wearing the red and white livery of the city stopped him at the gate. One of them came up to his horse and asked him his business.

"I'm a Guildsman," Dirk replied, pointing to the Iron Seal on his tunic. "I'm here to see Guildsergeant Bakker."

"The Guildhouse lies on *Victory Row*," one of the Guards said. "Do you know where that is?"

"Aye," Dirk replied, remembering the street from his youth.

The guard nearest him shouted up to the gatekeeper, who gave the order to raise the portcullis. The iron grate creaked as it rose, clicking into place when it reached the top.

"Be careful as you travel through town, sir," the Guard told him. "Rebel groups are everywhere. They target people like you."

"Thanks," Dirk replied. "I'll keep my eyes peeled,"

He passed through the egress onto the main thoroughfare.

The street packed with people, a vibrant mix of Humans and Elves. But unlike the shanty outside, none were poor or starving.

There was wealth here.

And as he made his way down the docks, it became clear why.

Ghis' location at the mouth of the River Rhund, meant that it was the last stop for any ship travelling through Gerwald on its way to the Middle Sea, and good coin could be made from supplying the vessels travelling through.

As he crossed the bridge that led to *Victory Square*, he saw the harbour bristling with the masts of a thousand crafts moored up along the jetties that lined the water's edge.

When he'd reached the other side, he rode his horse through the square, a huge plaza dedicated to the conquest of Gefghed, an event that had happened during the early days of Emperor's reign. A large statue stood at its centre, depicting the then young Monarch standing astride a diorama of the city, his legs spread either side of the Rhund.

A number of people were gathered around it, filling flasks and skeins from the pool at its base, among them a middle-aged man and his two sons, who were playing in the water.

Dirk found himself staring at them as he sidled past.

The man reminded him of his father; the pool, the lake, and the boy, a younger version of himself…

It was a picture of what his life could have been, if things had turned out differently.

All of a sudden there was a deafening bang.

Dirk's horse bucked and he was sent tumbling to the ground.

Picking himself up from the hard cobblestones, he saw that the statue had been blown asunder, its smooth bronze panels twisted into coiled steaming spikes. He glanced over to the people who had been sitting around its base. Many were lying on the ground, their motionless bodies covered in blood.

He looked around for the man and his children, but they were gone, blown to shreds by the force of the explosion.

As the ringing in his ears slowly dissipated, he began to hear the screams of the people all around, and he saw a number of men rushing forward to help the wounded.

Dirk rose to his feet and made his way towards them, still somewhat dazed by the blast.

To his left he heard shouting and yelling and turned his head to see a figure in a dark cloak running through the crowd.

Without a moment's hesitation he gave chase, following the man into a narrow alley that led off the main square. The bomber was quick and nimble, darting between the barrels and boxes that lined the passage. Halfway down, he stopped and climbed onto one of the barrels. Then he jumped up and grabbed the ledge of a window on the first floor.

"Stop!" Dirk ordered, as the man hauled himself up.

The assailant turned his head and looked at him. Through the shadows of the alley and under the darkness of the man's hood, Dirk glimpsed his ears. They were elongated and tipped with points.

He was an Elf.

Was he one of the Rebels?

Dirk rushed forward and leapt up onto the barrel in a single bound, stretching out his hand to seize the runner's ankle. His fingers touched the cloth of the Elf's slacks but slipped through the silken fabric.

An inch closer and he would have caught him....

Cursing his misfortune, he leapt up, took hold of the ledge, then hauled himself up and swung his leg over the sill.

Dropping down inside the room, he found a woman shivering in the corner.

"Where did he go?" Dirk rasped.

Trembling with fear, she pointed to the door.

Dirk gave her a nod then rushed through the egress.

Outside, he found himself standing in a long corridor of a tenement building. Many of the residents had opened their doors to see what was going on. A number of them were looking toward a staircase at the far end.

He raced over to it and glanced down the stairwell but saw no sign of his quarry. He looked up and saw a door swinging shut two storeys up. Taking hold of the balustrade he pulled himself up the stairs.

When he reached the top, he found that the door led out to a flat roof. He stormed out and began looking for the runner.

The Elf was nowhere to be seen.

Cursing under his breath, he turned back towards the door then suddenly caught a glimpse of movement to his right. He made his way towards it and saw a figure scaling the railings that surrounded the rooftop.

It was him.

He ran over, yelling at him to stop but the figure ignored him.

As Dirk got closer, he saw the Elf leap from the wall, his arms extended, like a diving swan.

Had he martyred himself?

Crashing up to the wall, he peered over the edge, half expecting to see the Elf's crumpled body on the street below.

But there was nothing there.

Where did he go?

He cursed and slammed his palm upon the rail.

Just then, his eyes detected movement on the roof of the adjacent building.

It was the Elf.

Instead of falling to his death, he'd somehow managed to jump across, and was now getting to his feet on the other side.

"Stop!" Dirk yelled.

The bomber looked up at him and flashed him a winning smile.

Dirk snorted through his nose.

The Elf bowed theatrically then made his way over to the other side of the roof, where he swung over the facade and took hold of the guttering beneath. Dirk watched impotently as he wrapped his arms around the leaden pipe and began sliding down to the street below.

It seemed his quarry had escaped

He grunted in frustration, not knowing what to do.

Scanning the scene below he noticed a large dumpster standing in the snickelway between the two buildings. It was overflowing with rubbish. If he could drop down and land inside it, he could make up the distance in seconds.

He glanced at the Elf and saw that he was nearly halfway

33

down the pipe. As soon as he reached the bottom, he would spin off down the next alleyway and escape.

It was now or never.

He climbed up onto the railing, extending his arms to steady himself as he teetered on the edge. Then he took a deep breath to compose himself, before stepping out into the abyss....

At once he was falling through the air, the wind gusting up beneath him. The bin was directly below, getting bigger and bigger as he plummeted down.

CRASH!

He opened his eyes.

He was still alive.

After quickly checking himself to make sure he wasn't hurt, Dirk stood up then waded through the debris, where he swung himself over the side and dropped down onto the pavement. The stench of the bin was revolting. It was full of rotting food.

Wiping the putrid gunk from his face, he glanced over to the alley and saw the Elf planting his feet at the bottom of the drainpipe.

The bomber looked shocked to see him.

It was clear he'd thought he'd escaped.

Dirk dashed toward him.

As expected, the Elf spun off down the passage. Dirk chased after him, driving his legs as fast as they could go.

The Elf glanced back and yelled a curse.

Dirk noticed that he was panting, out of breath.

He was nearly spent.

Just a few more yards and he would have him...

The bomber suddenly found an extra burst of pace. He reached the end of the passage and turned into the next street.

Hot on his heels, Dirk rounded the corner, and found himself in a crowded avenue that was home to a number of bars and taverns. He quickly scanned the scene and caught sight of the Elf dashing through the throng towards an Inn named 'The

Rebel's Pride'.

He darted after him, but the crowd slowed his pace.

Before long he realised that the people in the street were deliberately blocking his way.

"Guildsman," he shouted. "Let me through!"

The crowd didn't listen.

Instead, they came closer, and began boxing him in.

He stepped back to issue another challenge and was met with a murder of angry looks and unwelcome glares.

"Get back where you belong!" a voice shouted from within the mob.

"Yeah, piss off back to Gerwald, round-ears!"

At once he realised where he was.

The runner had led him into the *Weidenslosse,* the Elven district.

Dirk immediately held up his hands.

"Listen to me," he said. "I'm a Guildsman. I'm pursuing a criminal."

"We don't care," a She-Elf with a sullen face, retorted. "These are our streets. You're not welcome here."

Someone grabbed his shoulder from behind

Dirk turned his head and saw a huge brute standing over him. He swept away the thug's hand and raised his fists.

It was the wrong move.

The mob swarmed forward as one.

"Guild scum!" he heard someone shout.

A punch was thrown.

Remembering his training, Dirk turned inside the strike and responded with a jab. His knuckles connected with the attacker's windpipe and he dropped to the floor, clutching his neck.

Another punch was thrown from the left.

This one landed true, striking Dirk on the shoulder, but his pauldron absorbed the impact.

More hits then came in, this time from both sides at once, and he could do nothing more but to lift his arms and drop his chin to protect himself as they piled in.

Someone then seized his arm, pulling it away. Another person took his leg, and all of a sudden, Dirk was lifted into the air.

"Lynch him!" the mob roared as they carried him down the street toward a large tree.

Out of the corner of his eye, an Elf appeared from one of the doorways carrying a rope, which he was tying into a noose. He joined the crowd just before they threw Dirk down at the base of the trunk. Dazed and winded, the cord was placed over his head and the other end of the rope was then tossed up over one of the branches and caught by the Elves on the other side.

"Heave!" someone in crowd roared.

The Elves behind him pulled on the rope. The noose tightening around his neck and he was lifted up into the air. In a fit of panic, he began clawing at the cord with his fingers, but the more he poked and prodded the tighter it became.

He opened his mouth and gasped for air, but his lungs wouldn't fill.

He felt his face getting hotter and hotter.

He cried out but there was no sound.

The crowd began laughing and mocking him as he struggled on the line, his legs thrashing beneath him in a hangman's jig.

The world started to haze around him.

He knew that it wouldn't be long before he passed out.

Think, a voice inside his head told him.

Think, or you'll die....

He suddenly had an idea.

Reaching down, his hand found the hilt of the dagger at his belt and he drew it from its sheath. Through the fog of suffocation, he found the strength to lift the blade above his head and swipe at the line that was killing him.

CRACK!

He fell to the ground and landed in a crumpled heap. The rope around his neck immediately loosened and he clawed it away with his fingers.

He took in a deep breath.

The sudden rush of oxygen to his brain made him feel euphoric.

But he wasn't out of the woods yet...

He was still surrounded by the mob, and they were furious that he'd escaped.

The noose was re-tied, and they lifted him up, pulling back his head so they could slip it on. He shook himself free and dropped his chin, pressing it tightly against his collar. The Elf holding the rope smacked him on the back of the head, and with a roar, the mob joined in, kicking him in his sides and back.

Wilting under the barrage, Dirk dropped down onto the floor and curled himself up into a ball, covering his head with his hands.

As the fists and heels rained down on him, he heard the sound of marching feet behind him.

Oh no, he thought, *more of them...*

But his fears were quelled when someone shouted a warning.

"The Guard!" they yelled.

The kicking suddenly ceased.

Dirk parted his arms and saw the mob backed away as a forest of dark black boots enveloped him on either side. Glancing up he saw his red-and white shirted saviours stomping forward. They were armed with solid oak batons, which they swung at any Elf that got too close.

Dirk pushed himself up against the trunk of the tree and watched as they shunted the crowd further down the street.

"Are you ok, son?" a voice asked.

Dirk looked up and saw a middle-aged Guardsman standing over him.

"Aye," he nodded.

The man offered Dirk a hand and pulled him to his feet.

"Where's your partner?" he asked.

"I don't have one," Dirk replied. "

"In Ghis?" he exclaimed. "Are you mad?"

Dirk shook his head.

"I was in pursuit of a suspect," he replied, rubbing at his neck where the noose had dug into his skin. "But I lost him in the crowd."

"Who's your commander?" the man asked.

"I don't have one yet," Dirk replied.

The man gave him a curious look.

"I've only just arrived," he clarified, producing the document Patz had given him. "I've orders to meet Guildsergeant Bakker."

"Guildsergeant Bakker?" the man replied. "No wonder you have a death wish..."

Dirk dusted himself down and glanced at the mob, who were being kettled down the street by the soldiers

"Do you think you can you pick out the swines who did this to you?" the Guardsman asked.

Dirk scanned his eyes over the faces in the crowd.

"No," he replied. "I can't."

The man sniffed.

"Are you sure?" he asked.

Dirk shook his head.

"I honestly can't remember," he said. "It all happened so fast."

"Listen," the Guard said. ""There are a couple of villains in here that we've been after for a while... Maybe I could point them out for you to jog your memory?"

Dirk laughed.

"Is that how the law works down here?"

The Guard sniffed.

"Welcome to Ghis," he replied.

CHAPTER 4

The Ghisian Guildhouse was far more impressive than its counterpart in Royal Kronnig. In a former life, it had been a Kirk, an old one, built long before the establishment of V'Loirean Church. Dirk knew this as its roof was missing the standard crown of nine spires.

The structure was made entirely of stone, a useful material in a city as volatile as Ghis, where arson was frequent.

Stepping inside the iron braced doors, he found himself in a knave that had been converted into a reception area, where people could come to submit their warrants. A caged wire fence surrounded it, breached by a single locked door. A Guildsman sat at a small desk on the other side.

"Can I help you?" he asked as Dirk came forward.

"I'm here to sign up," Dirk replied. "I've been sent by Major Patz of the Royal Kronnig Guildschool."

He rolled up his scroll and slid it through the bars.

The man unfurled the parchment, studied it for a moment, then unlocked the interior door and beckoned him to enter.

"We don't get many *fresh bloods* down here," he said, as he handed back Dirk's papers. "I hope you know what you've let yourself in for."

Dirk rubbed his neck.

"I'm aware of the risks," he replied.

The sentry led him through the main hall, which contained rows of tables and chairs.

"This is our Mess," the man said, with a wave of his hand. "It's probably the best thing about this place."

"What's the worst?" Dirk asked.

"The heating," the man chuckled.

He led Dirk away to one of the side rooms then knocked upon its solid ashen door before walking away.

"Good luck with your new unit," he said.

"Aren't you going to introduce me?" Dirk replied.

The man shook his head.

"You're on your own from here," he remarked. "They don't take too kindly to outsiders... Even other Guildsmen."

His words didn't inspire confidence.

"Any advice on what I should say?" he asked.

The man sniffed.

"If you want to make an impression with this lot..." he replied. "Make it loud."

He shuffled back to his post, while Dirk waited by the door. A few moments later, he heard the latch being lifted on the other side. The door swung open. A dark-skinned Kulaanian stood on the other side. He was huge and wore a Guildsman's Uniform with the pattern of snake embroidered into its shoulders.

He gave Dirk a menacing look.

"I'm here to join your unit," he said in response, holding up his scroll.

The man appeared somewhat confused.

"I've a recommendation," Dirk said. "From Major Patz at the Guildschool."

Upon hearing the name, the big man nodded, then ushered him inside. Dirk stepped through and found himself in a large chamber lit by a series of lanterns fixed to the wall. The room had been partitioned into two sections: one containing a row of bunks; the other, a communal area, where there were desks, tables and chairs.

Sitting on the chairs were four other Guildsmen, who stopped and stared at him as he entered. Dirk noticed they were all wearing similar uniforms to the Kulaanian.

"Who the devil are you?" the first man said.

He was a northerner, blonde and fair-skinned.

"Guildsman Vanslow," Dirk answered. "I've come to see your Guildsergeant."

"Why's that?" the man sitting furthest away replied.

His skin was ruddier than the first man and his hair was jet-black. Dirk guessed that he was Grexian, though it was hard to tell from the man's accent. The Prutch he spoke sounded guttural, and somewhat bastardised.

"I've come to join your unit," Dirk replied.

"There's no room," the third man said.

Dirk fixed his eyes on the doughty figure sitting half-on, half-off the table. His physique was stunted, and he appeared short, as if he was a mongrel child of a Human and a Dwarf.

"I've a letter of recommendation," Dirk said, gesturing to the Kulaanian.

"We don't care," said the fourth man, who was distinguished from the rest by a long mane of blonde hair that trailed over his shoulders. "We don't accept recruits."

"I'm not a recruit," Dirk replied, pointing to the Iron Seal sewn into his tunic.

"You look like one," the Half-Dwarf laughed. "Are you even able to grow a beard?"

He chuckled, sending shivers through his grizzly jowls.

"Where's the Guildsergeant?" Dirk asked, ignoring the man's comment.

"We can get him for you if you like," the fair-skinned man said. "...But he'll only say the same."

"He only wants men who know how to handle themselves," the Grexian interjected. "Do you know how to fight?"

Dirk snorted.

"What is this?" he said. "A Guild or a pissing contest?"

The man with the long blonde hair laughed.

"He's serious," the fair-skinned man said.

"So am I," Dirk replied.

"A serious boy," the Half-Dwarf mocked.

"No," Dirk said. "I'm a Guildsman, the same as you."

"No," a voice said behind him. "You're not."

Dirk turned to see a middle-aged man walking towards him with the epaulettes of an officer.

"We're no ordinary Guildsman," he said, coming forward. "We're the Red Vipers."

His crown was balding, and the sides of his head were cropped short. He had the appearance of a northerner, but he wasn't an imperial. Dirk guessed Hessell or Hussfalt, as his voice was tinged with a Westren lilt.

"Guildsergeant Bakker?" Dirk said.

"Aye," the man replied. "And who are you?"

"Dirk Vanslow," he replied. "I'm here on the recommendation of Major Patz. He says you know him."

"I do," the man replied. "A brave man..."

He looked Dirk up and down.

"...But why he'd send me someone like you, I've no idea."

Dirk handed him the letter.

"There's no need," Bakker replied. "Like Varek told you, we don't take new bloods. Our work requires *experienced* men, warriors. Not children."

"I can handle myself," Dirk replied.

"Really?" Bakker laughed.

He leaned in close.

"I'll only say this once. Go home. This is not the place for you."

Dirk stepped back and held his gaze.

"I want to be here," he said.

Bakker smiled.

"Then prove it."

He pointed at the Kulaanian.

"If you can drop Mu'Ungo here, I'll consider your application. If not, you'll go back to wherever it is you came from and find more suitable employment."

"...Like wet nursing," the Grexian added.

The other men laughed.

Bakker chuckled and looked Dirk in the eye.

"Agreed?" he said.

Dirk glanced at the huge southerner standing before him. The man had at least a foot on him in terms of height and was considerably heavier.

He didn't stand a chance.

But he had no choice.

"Agreed," he replied.

Bakker stepped back and the other Guildsmen gathered round, dragging aside their table to make space in the middle of the room.

Mu'Ungo took off his tunic and threw it onto one of the bunks. As Dirk removed his shirt, he could sense the big man's unease.

He wasn't afraid, just tense.

It was clear he didn't want to fight.

Maybe he didn't think there was any sport in beating a man half his size?

Or maybe it was something else?

Once the two of them had stripped down to their slacks, the Half-Dwarf, who the others called 'Boors', stepped between them and held out his hand.

"Are you ready?" he asked.

Both of them nodded.

"Then fight!"

He dropped his hand and stepped back.

Immediately, the Kulaanian charged at him with his arms spread.

Knowing that it would be a mistake to try to stand his ground, Dirk ducked beneath his arm and spun behind him.

The big man stumbled to a halt. He turned round and glared at him, then beat the flat of his chest with his fist.

Letting out a frustrated grunt, he came at Dirk once again, this time more cautiously.

Dirk backed off, tracing the line of a semi-circle with his feet to avoid being trapped against the wall. Mu'Ungo stalked him slowly, aping his movements.

"Come on Dark One," the Guildsman with the long hair

shouted. "Stop messing around and drop him!"

Mu'Ungo reacted to the comment by bounding forward.

Dirk sidestepped to his right and his opponent butted the wall, to a chorus of laughter from his colleagues.

The Kulaanian spun round and growled, but beneath his fierce countenance Dirk saw a hint of sadness in his eyes. He got the impression that despite the big man's size and strength, he had a soft heart underneath.

Dirk stepped backwards into the centre of the room.

Mu'Ungo charged at him once again.

As before, Dirk sidestepped and ducked under his arms.

"V'Loire!" the Half-Dwarf cried.

"What are you playing at Blackskin," the Grexian yelled. "He's making you look like a fool."

His comment angered the Kulaanian and he spun round and came at Dirk with speed, seizing his arm.

He tried to yank it free but couldn't break the Southerner's powerful grip.

"That's it Mu'Ungo," the Half-Dwarf said. "Show him who's boss!"

The big man pulled him forward, and for the first time Dirk felt the man's true strength. Before he knew it, he was enveloped in the big man's arms.

The Kulaanian then tightened his clench and Dirk felt the air being squeezed from his lungs. Trapped, and lacking the strength to resist, he was ready to concede defeat.

But then all of a sudden, he heard a whispering in his ear.

"Arm drop..." the voice said.

In his delirium Dirk thought he was hearing things but then he realised that the words had been spoken by his opponent, and what's more, they were an instruction, for an 'Arm Drop' was a technique he'd learned in his wrestling class. It involved locking an opponent's upper arm then drawing them over an outstretched leg. Designed for close quarter fighting, it was the textbook counter to a bear hug.

Following his opponent's advice, Dirk extended his right

leg and bracketed his calf against the big man's shin. He then twisted his body a half step to the left. Though he was tiny in comparison to the big man, the shift of weight was enough to displace him, and with his right leg trapped, he had nowhere left to go but down.

Dirk twisted as he fell, holding on to the big man's arm.

Mu'Ungo hit the floor with a crash.

Dirk landed on top.

He looked up to see the faces of the men who were watching.

None of them believed what they were seeing.

The Half-Dwarf slammed his fist into the table; the man with the long hair looked up to the heavens; the Grexian visibly tutted, and the fair-skinned northerner shook his head in disbelief.

The only one not to react was Bakker, whose face remained impassive, and Dirk watched as he slowly raised his hands and began striking his palms together in applause.

With the fight now over, Dirk released his grip on the opponent's arm and got to his feet. He then turned and offered his hand, but under the glare of his colleagues, the big man refused to shake it.

"Well done," Bakker said moving forward. "You bested our strongest."

"I guess that means I'm in." Dirk said.

"Not so fast…" Bakker said.

He came forward and held Dirk's gaze.

The man's stare unnerved him, as if he was looking inside his soul.

"Right now, all I see is potential," Bakker sneered, "…To truly be one of us, you'll need to prove yourself in the field."

He turned and looked at the fair-skinned man.

"Varek," he said. "Take him out with you tonight…"

He gave the man a crooked smile.

"…Show him how we do things in Ghis."

Varek nodded.

"And take him to a bathhouse on your way back," he added. "He smells like rotten fish."

CHAPTER 5

Dirk and Varek set off from the Guildhouse, turning down *Victory Row* into the square, which was swarming with the city guard following the bombing.

"Vandal scum," Varek remarked as they passed the ruined sculpture. "The ones who did this deserve to be hanged."

Dirk glanced at the bloodstains surrounding the statue's base. It was hard to disagree.

"If you ask me," the fair-haired man continued. "The only good Elf is a dead Elf."

This he was less certain of.

Then again, nothing he'd seen thus far proved things otherwise.

"Do we know what explosive was used by the bomber?" Dirk asked.

"Firepowder, most likely," the man replied, as they stepped onto the bridge. "They've been stealing shipments of it from the dockside warehouses...."

He pointed across the way to a large storage depot that stood behind the pontoon.

"When's the next one due?" Dirk asked.

"Two nights from now," Varek replied.

"Do you think they'll raid it?"

"We're counting on it," the man replied with a smile.

Dirk gave him a curious look.

"We've laid a trap for them," he explained. "We're moving the barrels to the South side Depot. When the Elves show up at the northern one, they'll find nothing inside but Guildsmen."

"Clever," Dirk remarked.

"We need to be," Varek insisted. "These Elves may be sub-human, but they're not stupid."

"What if the raid doesn't happen?"

Varek smiled cruelly.

"We've already got that covered."

They crossed the bridge and made their way Westwards along the harbourside, passing a row of Tavernas that stood at the edge of the boardwalk. Despite the hour, the place was heaving with people, mostly sailors, who were drinking outside on the verandas.

"These are the loyalist haunts," Varek commented. "For Humans... and Elves that know their place. South of the river is where all the troublemakers live."

"I think I've been there," Dirk replied.

His neck was still sore.

"The *Weidenslosse*," Varek said. "We call it *Rebels Row*... The City Guard are based there in the Citadel to keep an eye on things, but sometimes they call on us to help when things get... testy."

Dirk knew from his training that the *Guild of Finders* were not responsible for keeping the peace. That obligation fell on the local guard or militia. The Guild's role was to conduct investigations into unsolved crimes and bring wanted men to Justice. Though the two organisations often worked together, the Guild's independent status prevented any kind of formal assimilation.

"The people there don't seem very happy with the Guild," Dirk remarked.

"They hate us," Varek replied. "But that's ok, because we hate them back."

"I thought the Guild was supposed to be neutral?" Dirk said.

Varek sniffed.

"Try being neutral when they murder your family," he replied.

Dirk said nothing.

He knew exactly how it felt.

They continued along the harbour until they came to an Inn that stood at the far end of the dock.

"Fancy going in?" Varek asked.

"But we're on duty," Dirk replied.

"Don't worry," Varek said. "This isn't a social visit."

Dirk followed him up the steps onto the veranda, where a sign hung from the awning that read 'Ruyven's Rums'.

"Are you ready for your first test?" Varek said, placing his hand on the door.

Dirk nodded.

"Good," the man replied, then pushed it ajar and made his way inside.

The musty smell of long-dried liquor invaded Dirk's nostrils as they crossed the threshold into a dimly lit room with exposed wooden joists. Several patrons were sitting at a nest of tables opposite the bar, which stood facing the door. Many of the men looked like aged seafarers, their long beards curling up underneath the collars of their salt-stained jackets.

One of them caught Dirk's eye and sneered at him above the smoke of his pipe. On his table were a row of empty shot glasses and a bottle of Colony Red: a strong Rum that originated from Tibrut.

Varek ignored their stares and went straight to the bar, where he rang the small service bell that sat on the counter. Dirk heard a shuffling of feet in the room behind the bar and moments later a middle-aged Elf came out to greet them.

He assumed it was the owner, the eponymous *Ruyven* of *Ruyven's Rums,* and his suspicions were confirmed when Varek addressed him.

"Ruyven," he said, with a friendly smile. "How's business?"

"Not bad," the Elf replied sullenly.

"And your son?"

"He's well," Ruyven replied.

Dirk noticed the unease in his voice.

He seemed tense and guarded.

"Ruyven's boy joined the City Guard," Varek declared loudly.

He turned back to the Innkeeper.

"You're very proud of him, aren't you?"

Ruyven nodded.

"He's doing well," the Elf noted.

"It can't be easy for him, though..." Varek continued. "...What with him being the only Point-Ear to wear the Red and White..."

"He doesn't mind," Ruyven replied. "He loves serving his country."

"Which one?" Varek pressed. "Gerwald or Veleenum?"

His words were laced with sarcasm. It was clear that Varek was implying Ruyven's son was a spy.

"Do you gentleman want a drink?" Ruyven asked, steering the conversation away. "I'm getting weekly deliveries of *Einhof Sweet* now - they say it's the best Rum in the Empire."

"You know what?" Varek said. "I think I'd like to try some of your special brands instead. You know, the ones you keep out back."

Ruyven cut his eyes at the man.

"Of course," he said finally. "This way, please."

He led them through the bar to a room at the back, which was stocked full of barrels containing rare and exquisite rums from across the known world.

"So, what is it you really want?" Ruyven said, as he stepped into the centre of the room.

"Information," Varek replied.

The Elf shook his head.

"I've nothing to say," he replied. "Like I told you before, my Rebel days are over."

Varek smiled.

"Ruyven used to run with the Swords of Sheenah," he said to Dirk. "He's killed many a Human in his day..."

"That was a long a time ago," the Elf replied coldly.

"...So you keep telling us," Varek responded.

"I was young and impressionable back then," Ruyven explained. "I was led astray; made to believe things that weren't true..."

"Like Gefghed belongs to the Elves?" Varek suggested.

The Elf's eyes drifted to the floor.

"See," he said, glancing at Dirk. "Old habits die hard."

"I may still believe in the cause," the Innkeep admitted. "But it should be achieved through peaceful means, without bloodshed."

Varek's lips parted into a wicked smile.

"Sure," he said. "Like that's going to happen..."

"Listen," the Elf said, stepping back. "I don't know what you want but whatever it is, I can't give it to you. Like I said, those days are over..."

"So you have nothing to do with your old crew?"

"No," Ruyven replied.

Varek turned to Dirk.

"He's lying," he said.

"I'm not," Ruyven insisted. "Why would I risk it? I have a life now, a family, a business..."

Varek crooked his neck and looked into the man's eyes.

"So what was Olojeon Hax doing here last night?"

Ruyven looked stunned.

"I know nothing of that," he said, the words tumbling from his lips.

"Orc shit," Varek replied.

He stepped forward and punched the man in the stomach.

Ruyven bent double and fell to his knees.

"Please," he groaned. "I'm telling the truth."

Varek hit him around the face with the flat of his palm.

A spittle of blood sprayed from his mouth, staining the barrels a deep shade of red.

"Don't lie to me," Varek snarled, taking the Elf by his hair and slamming his head against the nearest cask.

"What are you doing?" Dirk spat.

"What does it look like?" Varek replied. "I'm interrogating

the witness."

"It doesn't look like interrogation to me," Dirk remarked.

Varek turned and glared at him.

"We both know he's lying," he said.

Dirk shook his head.

"Maybe he's telling the truth?"

Varek laughed.

"You hear that?" he said to Ruyven. "He thinks you're innocent."

He kicked the Elf in the ribs.

"Stop..." he groaned. "Please...."

Varek reach for the dagger at his belt, but Dirk seized his wrist before he could draw it.

"Don't," he said. "This isn't right."

"This is Ghis," Varek snorted. "We do things different here."

He pushed away Dirk's hand and drew the blade. Then he knelt down beside the stricken Elf and held the knife up to his face.

"Last chance," he said.

The Elf shook his head.

Varek responded by thrusting the point of his blade into the sides of the nearest cask. He then pulled it out and a stream of rum began leaking from it. The man stood up and did the same to the barrels that were stacked above.

"No..." Ruyven wept. "Not my stock... Without this place, I'll have nothing."

He leant up against the casks and began plugging the holes with his palms.

"You'll still have your son..." Varek said, rising to his feet.

His lips parted into a cruel grin.

"...But I'm sure we can change that."

"What do you mean?" Ruyven said.

"I don't know..." Varek mused. "Maybe I could speak to his commander.... Tell him who his father is?"

"No..." Ruyven replied. "You wouldn't..."

"Why not?" Varek sneered. "You could say it's my civil duty."

"Please," he begged. "They'll kill him..."

"Yes," the Guildsman sighed. "That's what happens to trai-tors."

Dirk saw Ruyven's eyes drift to the floor, defeated.

"Ok..." he said. "I admit it... Hax was here, I spoke to him."

Varek gave Dirk a knowing look.

"See," he said. "I told you."

The man reached down and hauled the Elf up by his collar.

"So what did you talk about?"

"Firepowder," Ruyven replied. "They're running low."

"Tell me something I don't know," Varek sneered.

"He asked me to watch the warehouses," the Elf said, "...keep tabs on the number of guards."

"And what did you say?"

"I refused," Ruyven replied. "Like I told you, I'm not a Rebel anymore."

"So you keep telling us," Varek scoffed. "What else did he say?"

The Elf shook his head.

"Nothing. I gave him my answer and he left."

"Where was he heading?" Dirk asked.

The Elf looked up at him.

"I don't remember," he replied.

Varek snorted through his nose then thrust his blade into another keg.

"Does this jog your memory?"

Ruyven shook his head.

Varek stabbed another.

"Shafarr," he muttered. "He was heading to Shafarr..."

"Shafarr?" Varek replied. "Why there?"

"It's where they store their supplies," he said, holding his head in his hands. "But please, no more. That's all I know, I swear!"

Varek turned to Dirk.

"I think that's enough for us to go on," he said, curling his lip.

He looked back at the Elf.

"But if it turns out you've lied to us," he warned "We'll be back for you... And your son."

He turned and left the room.

Dirk stepped back and Ruyven glanced up at him, his eyes filled with tears.

Holding his breath, he backed away then followed Varek through the bar.

"Was all that necessary?" he asked, as they stepped out onto the veranda.

"I'd say so" Varek replied. "We learned the location of the Rebel stores."

"Only because you tortured him," Dirk said.

"So?" Varek replied.

"It's against our code," Dirk said.

The man glared at him.

"Down here, there is no code," he said. "The sooner you realise that the better..."

* * *

After stopping by a bathhouse, Dirk and Varek returned to the Guild and found that the others were already in their bunks. Most of them were sleeping but Mu'Ungo was lying awake, nursing a bloodied nose.

"You'll sleep there," Varek said, pointing to a bed opposite the Kulaanian. "Get some rest. Tomorrow's going to be a long day."

Dirk made his way over to the cot, took off his tunic and placed it under his pillow. He then laid himself down and turned onto his side. His eyes met those of the Kulaanian, who averted his gaze.

"I'm sorry if I hurt you earlier," Dirk whispered.

"You didn't," the big man replied. "This happened later."

"How?" Dirk asked.

Mu'Ungo didn't answer.

He didn't need to.

It was clear his colleagues had done it.

As Dirk closed his eyes, he couldn't help but feel sorry for the big man. It was obvious he was being victimised by the others, probably because he was different.

He buried his face into the pillow and waited for the face of the one-eyed Elf to appear in his mind's eye.

The figure had haunted his dreams each night for the past six years.

Things were be different now though.

Now the face had a name.

And its name was Araxys…

CHAPTER 6

The next morning Dirk woke to the sound of his unit getting ready for breakfast. After putting on his uniform, he followed them out to the mess hall, where a food counter had been set up in the apse.

A number of Guildsmen from other units were waiting in a line, but quickly moved out of the way when they saw the Vipers approaching.

"Lions before Lambs," Kort sneered as he led them to the front.

After loading up his plate, Dirk joined his unit at a table in the far corner. While he was eating, he couldn't help but notice that the Guildsmen of the other units refused to look at them.

"What's with them?" Dirk asked. "Why won't they sit with us?"

"We won't let them," Boors answered.

"Why not?" Dirk said.

"Because they're unworthy," Kort, explained. "They're cowards, who lack mettle..."

As he spoke, he glanced at Varek, who replied with a knowing nod.

"They're weak," he added. "They wear the seal, but they lack the iron."

The men laughed, but it was clear they'd heard the line before.

After finishing their food, they returned to their Quarters, where Guildsergeant Bakker was waiting for them. He was standing in front of a large map of Gefghed that had been fixed to the wall, and as they came in, he beckoned them to sit.

"Morning briefing…" Varek said, as he pushed past Dirk and took a chair at the front. Kort, Ermus, Boors and Mu'Ungo then took the seats behind him. With nowhere left to sit Dirk had no option but to stand.

Once everyone was settled, Bakker began.

He skipped the pleasantries and got straight to the point.

"Last night," he said, "We acquired information that the Swords of Sheenah were using the village of Shafarr to store their weapons and explosives."

He gave Varek a nod of thanks then gestured toward the map.

"The village lies here…" he said, pointing to its location. "…At the edge of a gorge approximately five miles south of Shemali."

Bakker traced an imaginary line on the parchment, which indicated the route of their journey from Ghis.

"We'll divert off the main road, here, to avoid being seen in the town," he said.

He stepped forward and turned to face his troops.

"As you all know, Shafarr is deep inside Rebel Country," he said. "So be prepared for anything."

Dirk glanced at the faces of his colleagues.

None of them displayed any signs of fear.

They appeared eager and determined, as if they relished the challenge.

He ordered the unit to make ready for their journey, and once everyone had packed their things, he marched them out to the stables. To Dirk's surprise, he saw his grey stallion waiting for him in one of the stalls.

"We found him wondering the Square after yesterday's bombing," the farrier said, as Dirk stepped forward and patted Mott's nose. "When we noticed the Guild seal on his saddle, we brought him here."

"Thanks," Dirk said.

He tickled the stallion beneath its chin.

"Did you miss me, boy?"

Mott snorted happily.

He climbed up into the saddle and coaxed him forward, bringing him into line with the mounts.

Once all the riders were ready, Bakker signalled for the gate to be opened. He then led them out, turning right down Victory Row towards the Southern Gate. After passing through it they then turned east onto the Shemali Road.

From what he'd seen on the map, Dirk estimated that it would take at least half-a day to get to the village, and their journey would be a difficult one, covering many miles of rough terrain.

The sun shone hotter as the day went on, the temperature only cooling as they began their ascent into the hills.

At the crest of a small ridge that overlooked the town of Shemali, Bakker ordered the unit to turn off the main road and make their way through the desert, so they could enter the village from the south.

"They may have watchers on the road," he warned, "so we'll approach from where they least expect it. It'll give them less chance to prepare..."

They left the path and travelled southeast across the arid, barren landscape. The air here was much drier than it was in the city and made drier still by the frequent blasts of wind that swept sand up into their faces.

After an hour so of riding, Ermus, who was travelling at the front of the column, signalled that he'd spotted the village and jockeyed his horse back to the group.

"It's there," he told them. "Just beyond that ridge."

Bakker called everyone together.

"Remember the plan," he said. "Come in hard and fast, leaving them no time to react."

He pointed to Ermus, Boors and Kort.

"Once we're in, you three gather up the villagers and hold them in the square while Varek and I search the dwellings to the West..."

He turned to Mu'Ungo.

"...You and Dirk will take the houses to the East. Is every-thing clear?"

The men nodded in agreement.

"And remember," he said. "We don't know who else is watching us, so keep your eyes peeled..."

He drew his sword then turned his horse in the direction of the village.

"Are you ready?" he asked them.

His men answered with a collective grunt.

"Then let's do this..."

He spurred his mare forward towards the ridge, and his troops fell in behind him.

* * *

When they reached the edge of the gorge, Dirk glanced down at the settlement of Shafarr below. Nestled in the shadow of the ridgeline, the township was comprised of no more than twenty buildings, which had been arranged in a broken semi-circle around a small square. At its centre stood a twisted obelisk that resembled a pinecone. Dirk remembered learning of such things in his theology classes and knew it to be ancient monolith dedicated to the Elven Goddess.

"Ride!" Bakker yelled, urging his steed down the slope. His mare whinnied in defiance, relenting only after he'd tapped its thighs with the flat of his blade. It stumbled over the edge then thundered down the cliff side. The steeds of the other men followed, one after the other, until all six of them were streaming down the slope.

As they neared the bottom, Dirk saw the town's inhabitants darting towards their hovels, their faces ashen with fear. A chorus of screams then filled the air as Bakker's mount crossed the plaza, rounding up those who were too slow in their retreat.

"Quickly," Bakker ordered, as Varek drew up alongside him. "Raid the houses."

Together they dismounted and approached the door of

59

the nearest house. The younger man lifted his boot and struck it with his heel, splintering its frame. With his sword raised, Bakker stepped inside and barked orders at the occupants to leave. A thin-looking male Elf emerged, clutching his children. Varek took him by the collar and ushered him toward Kort, who was standing in the middle of the square with his crossbow.

Dirk climbed down from his saddle and made his way over to the furthest house on the right. Mu'Ungo joined him as he stepped up onto the veranda, and the Kulaanian banged at the door with his huge fist, shaking it on its hinges.

It was more than enough to scare its inhabitants into compliance, and Dirk watched as the door swung open and a woman and small child came out.

"Go to the obelisk," Dirk said. "Do as we say, and you won't be harmed."

With tears welling in her eyes, the She-Elf nodded and dragged her daughter to the centre of the square, where Boors and Ermus ordered them both to kneel.

"Guildsmen," Dirk shouted into the open door. "If anyone else is inside, come out now."

When no one responded, he gave Mu'Ungo a nod then crossed the threshold, leading with point of his blade.

After checking behind the door, Dirk quickly scanned the room and saw that it was empty save for a few basic items of furniture.

"Clear!" he yelled.

The Southerner stormed in behind him.

After searching the room and finding nothing, the two of them moved out and approached the second house.

The door opened as soon as they stepped onto its porch.

A young male Elf came out, holding up his hands.

"Please," he pleaded, "Don't kill me."

He dropped to his knees before them.

Dirk gestured to Mu'Ungo, who lifted him up by the nape of his collar and thrust him toward the growing body of people gathered in the square.

After checking the house and finding it was empty, Dirk and Mu'Ungo moved onto the third.

This time, the door was locked.

"Open up," Dirk yelled through the window. "This is a raid."

"Go away!" shouted a woman from inside. "You've no business being here."

"Open up…" Dirk repeated, "…Or we'll have to break down your door."

"Try it," the woman roared.

Dirk sighed then charged the frame with his shoulder. The force of impact shook the panel, but it didn't break.

"Let me," Mu'Ungo said.

Dirk stepped back and the big man shunted the door with his mighty shoulder. With an ugly crunch, the wood split asunder, smashing a hole in the uppermost quadrant.

Dirk peered in and saw that it had been barred on the inside with a thick wooden beam. He reached in to slide it away but as he did, he felt a sharp sting on the flesh of his forearm.

He yelped and withdrew his limb.

A silver needle used for knitting was embedded in the muscle above his wrist.

Gritting his teeth, he pulled it out then savagely kicked apart the remainder of the door with the heel of his boot.

Lifting up his *Hunter's Bite*, he stepped inside and found an old woman cowering beneath the window.

Mu'Ungo came in and seized her by the shoulder. She screamed and clawed at his wrists.

"Leave me be!" she yelled. "I've done nothing wrong."

"Then why are you hiding?" Dirk asked.

The She-Elf shook her head.

"This is my house," she spat. "You've no right to be here."

Mu'Ungo lifted her up and held her against the wall. Instinctively, he raised his arm to strike her.

"No," Dirk said, staying his hand.

The Kulaanian responded with a look of incredulity.

Dirk stepped forward and took the woman by the collar.

"Listen," he told her. "We're not here to play games. Either you tell me what's going on or I'll walk out of this room and leave you here with my friend?"

The woman looked up at the giant standing before her and visibly gulped.

"Ok," she said. "I'll talk…"

But before she could open her mouth to speak, they heard shouting and yelling outside.

Dirk turned and looked toward the sound.

Something was going on.

He gestured to Mu'Ungo to take the woman outside, and he took her by the neck and began frogmarching her over to the door.

As Dirk followed them out, he caught sight of Varek in the centre of the square, dragging a man across the ground by his hair. Bakker was following him.

"Bind him to the Obelisk," the Guildsergeant ordered.

Dirk glanced to his right and saw Boors at the saddle of his horse, retrieving a length of rope from his saddlebags.

"What's going on?" Dirk asked, as he moved forward with Mu'Ungo and the woman.

"Bakker found a locked trapdoor in one of the houses," Ermus sneered. "But he wouldn't give up the key."

Dirk watched as Kort held the man in place while Boors bound him to the block, groaning loudly as the cord was pulled tightly around his chest.

Bakker then approached the stricken man and slapped him across the face. He then punched the man in the stomach and kneed him in the groin.

The Elf gasped in pain.

Dirk instinctively stepped forward but Varek, who came up to him and bunted him in the chest.

"Don't even think about it," he said.

Dirk backed up and stood alongside Mu'Ungo and the She-Elf.

"If you know where it is," Dirk whispered to her, "I'd strongly advise you tell us."

"We don't have it," she whispered back, "The Rebels took it with them..."

"Guildsergeant," he yelled.

The officer ceased his barrage and looked at him.

"What is it, Dirk?" he growled.

"They don't have it," he replied.

Bakker smiled.

"Is that what they told you?" he laughed.

Boors and Ermus chuckled.

"Shut up," Varek rasped. "You're making a fool of yourself."

Bakker returned to the shackled Elf and drew the dagger from his belt. He placed the blade against the man's throat.

"Enough of this," he said. "Where's the key?"

"We don't have it..." the Elf groaned.

Bakker shook his head.

"Wrong answer."

In a single swift motion, he drew its razored edge across the Elf's windpipe. The villager gasped, and for a second nothing happened. Then suddenly the wound revealed itself as a stream of claret gushed down his chest. The sight was met with cries of horror from the twenty or villagers gathered before them. Some dropped to their knees and started wailing. Others baulked and turned away.

Bakker stepped forward and addressed them.

"Look at him, all of you..." he roared. "This is what happens when you try to resist us."

With his free hand, he lifted up the dying Elf's head, and a sickening gargle emanated from the hole in his throat; it was an ungodly rasping sound, as if he if was trying to breathe through the gash in his windpipe. The stricken Elf coughed, spitting blood over the villagers who were standing at the front. It was a truly horrifying moment and the sight of it caused one of the older She-Elves to faint.

When the gurgling finally ceased, Bakker withdrew his

hand and the Elf's lifeless head dropped forward.

"So," he declared. "Anyone ready to tell me the truth?"

The crowd responded with a collective whimper.

Bakker snorted through his nose.

"Fine," he rasped. "Bring me another..."

Dirk watched as Boors seized the nearest villager to him, a young She-Elf, who looked no older than thirteen. She screamed in panic as he grabbed her by the neck and shunted her toward the block.

Dirk shook his head in disbelief at what was happening.

It was clear that the villagers didn't have the key, but Bakker was willing to execute them regardless.

Ermus dragged away the dead Elf's corpse as Boors brought her to the block.

"Please don't do this," the young woman begged, "Please.... We don't know where it is..."

Bakker nodded to Boors, who pushed her up against the stone. She whimpered uncontrollably as the rope was wound around her body, fixing her in place.

Bakker cast his eyes over the villagers standing in front of him.

"This is your last chance," he warned.

When no one spoke, he shook his head then approached the woman with his dagger raised.

Dirk saw red.

He couldn't let this happen.

This was wrong.

He glanced at Varek, who responded with a smirk.

Dirk smirked back at him then suddenly charged forward, butting him with his shoulder. The fair-haired Guildsman groaned and crashed down onto his back. Dirk stepped over him and raced toward the She-Elf.

Bakker saw him coming.

He gestured to Ermus and Boors, and the two men barred his path. Dirk tried to dodge past them, but they tackled him to the ground.

He hit the floor hard.

At once, the Half-Dwarf was upon him.

Dirk punched up, striking the Half-Dwarf in the face, but the mongrels' thick skull absorbed the blow. He hit him again, but his time Boors caught his fist and twisted it to the side.

Dirk shrieked and brought up his other hand but Ermus grabbed his wrist and pinned it to the floor under his knee.

Trapped and immobilised, Dirk could do nothing more than curse them through gritted teeth.

"Bring him here," Bakker ordered.

The men lifted him up and marched him over to the obelisk.

"You just broke the Vow of Duty, lad," the Guildsergeant said.

"And you broke the Vow of Honour," Dirk replied. "You can't execute innocent people."

Bakker gestured towards the villagers.

"These people aren't innocent," he replied. "They're Rebels..."

He glanced at their faces.

"...All of them."

"They're civilians," Dirk replied. "They don't know anything."

"Well see about that," Bakker said.

"If they knew something," Dirk argued, "Don't you think they'd have said something by now?"

The Guildsergeant smiled.

"You underestimate them" he replied. "They're fanatics. And the lips of fanatics only part with pain."

Dirk shook his head.

"You're sick," he said.

Bakker smiled.

"I'm practical," he replied.

"He's not cut out for this," Varek sneered as he walked over.

Boors nodded in agreement.

"Oh no," Bakker said, shaking his head. "He's not weak..."

He paced forward and looked Dirk in the eye.

"There's steel in him. I saw it when I first looked into his eyes."

He ran his thumb across the blade of his knife.

"Who did they kill, boy?" he whispered. "Your mother? Your brother?"

"My father..." Dirk finished.

Bakker lips parted into a cruel smile.

"Bring him here..." he said.

Boors and Ermus shunted him forward.

"...Let him go."

The two men released his arms but stood close enough behind him to bar his escape.

Bakker palmed his dagger and handed it to Dirk.

"Kill her," he said. "Claim your place among us."

Dirk's heart skipped a beat.

He glanced around him and saw the other Guildsmen nodding.

"Go on," Kort urged. "Prove yourself."

Dirk hesitated, unsure whether or not to take the blade.

He knew deep down that they were his best hope of finding his father's killer... But to keep them onside, he'd have to become a murderer himself.

He was torn, was conflicted.

He didn't know what to do.

The hilt of Bakker's dagger touched his palm and his wrapped his fingers around it.

The knife trembled in his hand.

The She-Elf whimpered.

Bakker smiled.

"Do it," he said.

Dirk glanced at the She-Elf and at once saw the face of Araxys.

He brought the blade down at speed.

The crowd gasped.

THUNK!

He looked up and saw the She-Elf's face.

Her eyes were focused on the blade, which had struck the rock two inches from her ear.

The villagers let out a collective sigh of relief.

Dirk dropped the knife at his feet.

Bakker glared at him.

He'd failed their test.

"No," Dirk muttered. "This isn't who I am..."

The Guildsergeant shook his head, his face a picture of disappointment.

"Such a shame," he replied. "You had so much promise."

He gestured to the Ermus and Boors, who seized him by the arms.

"Mu'Ungo," Bakker shouted, "Watch over this craven while we finish up here."

The Kulaanian nodded and made his way forward while Boors and Ermus took his weapons. Then they handed him over to the big man, who began marching him to the edge of the square.

"Why didn't you do anything?" he asked, as Mu'Ungo stopped him near the horses.

"I owe him everything," he replied. "He brought me my freedom."

"How's that working out for you?" Dirk replied.

Mu'Ungo slapped him across the head then forced him down onto his knees.

He looked up to see Bakker standing over the dagger. He picked it up and placed it against the She-Elf's throat.

"No more lies," he said. "Where's the key?"

The young girl shook her head.

The Guildsergeant looked at her indignantly.

Dirk closed his eyes.

He couldn't watch...

"Wait!" someone shouted.

Dirk looked toward the crowd and saw an old man raising his hand.

"Don't kill her," he said. "I have it. It's here."

Bakker signalled to Varek, who barged through the crowd and seized the man by the collar and brought him to the fore.

"Please," the old man begged. "She's my granddaughter. She's all I have left."

"The key..." Bakker said.

The man reached inside his tunic and pulled out a large brass key that was attached to a length of cord.

The Guildsergeant swiped it from his hand and tossed it to Ermus.

"Open the trapdoor," Bakker said. "Bring out whatever they're hiding."

The longhaired Guildsman grinned then jogged over to the first hut. As he disappeared inside, Bakker glanced at Dirk and smiled victoriously.

Nothing needed to be said.

His point had been proven.

Dirk averted his gaze.

He wouldn't have murderers mocking him.

A few minutes later, Ermus emerged from the house carrying a large metal box.

"I've found something," he declared, bringing it to Bakker and placing it on the floor at his feet.

The Guildsergeant grinned, then gestured to Kort to release the She-Elf. Once he'd cut the ropes, she quickly ran over to the old man and embraced him in her arms.

Bakker stared at the box.

"What's inside?" he asked.

The old man hesitated before speaking.

"Coin..." he replied. "It's the war fund, sent by Veleenum to aid the cause."

"The *Cause*," Bakker sniffed.

He pointed to the box.

"When are you expecting them to come for this?"

The old man shook his head.

"We don't know," he said. "They only show up when they

need something."

"And when were they here last?"

"Three nights ago," he answered.

"All of them?" Bakker said.

"No," the old man replied. "Just one."

"Hax?" Varek offered.

He sighed and nodded.

"What did he want?" Bakker asked.

"He asked us if they could keep their Firepowder in our stores," the old man replied.

"Firepowder?" Bakker said.

He glanced at Varek, who replied with a smug grin.

"They didn't take any coin?"

"No," the old man replied. "It's all still there."

"How much?" Boors asked.

"We don't know," the Elf replied. "It's not ours to spend."

Bakker crouched down and looked at the box.

"Is it booby-trapped?" he asked.

"No."

Bakker stood up.

"Prove it."

He gestured to Varek, who brought the man forward and forced his down onto the ground in front of the casket.

Bakker and the other Vipers stepped back as the Elf flipped the catch and opened the lid.

A sparkle of gold dazzled in the sunlight.

Drawn to the gleam, Boors came forward, pushing the old man aside.

"How much is in there?" Kort asked.

"Thousands," the Half-Dwarf replied.

"We'll add it to the retirement fund," Bakker laughed.

Dirk was sickened.

Not only were his unit errant Guildsmen, but they were also common thieves.

"What'll you do with your cut?" Dirk asked Mu'Ungo sarcastically.

The Kulaanian didn't answer.

His silence suggested he wasn't happy about it either.

Bakker turned and addressed his men.

"Ermus," he began, "raze this place to the ground."

A collective gasp went up from the crowd.

"Kort, Varek..." he continued, "Take the prisoners into the desert and set them to work digging holes."

Dirk knew what that meant.

He was planning to execute them all.

In a twisted way, it made sense.

No survivors, no witnesses.

A number of the Elves in the crowd realised what was going on and began panicking.

"What kind of scum are you?" one of them shouted. "You're going to kill us all?"

"You sided with the Rebels," Bakker replied, "The punishment for treason is death."

As Kort and Varek began corralling the crowd, Bakker went over to his horse.

"Load the coin onto the horses," he said, unclipping his saddlebag and throwing it to Boors. "I want us out of here by nightfall."

The Half-Dwarf caught it and gave him a nod. Then he got down on his knees and began spooning the coin inside.

Dirk suddenly noticed the older Elf backing away.

He clutched his granddaughter and covered her ears.

It was a strange reaction.

Almost as if it was...

BANG!

Dirks ears rang from the blast.

He opened his eyes to find the square filled with a cloud of dark smoke. The Half-Dwarf emerged from the fog, holding out his arms in front of him... But at the end of his wrists were two bloody stumps.

His hands were missing, blown clean off by the blast.

He staggered forward then fell dead at Bakker's feet.

The Guildsergeant roared with rage.

"Kill them!" he yelled. "Kill them all!"

The square erupted into a mass panic.

Villagers began running to and fro, Guildsmen slashing at them with their swords.

Women were screaming, children were crying, and men were yelling murder.

In the chaos, several of the townsfolk broke away from the group and began running in the direction of the gorge.

Mu'Ungo saw them and removed his hand from Dirk's shoulder to reach for his blade.

Dirk seized his chance.

At once he tilted back his head then stood up straight, butting the Kulaanian beneath the chin. The force was enough to unsteady the big man and Dirk quickly spun on his heels and pushed him to the ground. As he fell, he dropped his sword and Dirk snatched it up before running over to his horse.

He quickly climbed up into the saddle and dug his heels into Mott's sides. The horse snorted then thundered forward, heading toward the crevasse.

As he raced away, Dirk heard Bakker yelling in the square.

"Get him!" he screamed. "Kill the traitor!"

CHAPTER 7

The hot air in the chasm blasted Dirk's face as he drove his horse hard over the dried-up riverbed. Looking back, he saw the outlines of the five riders chasing him, the thundering hooves of their steeds, shrouding them in a thin cloud of dust.

Up ahead, the canyon veered to the right. He steered his horse into the turn. Mott was panting with exertion. They'd rode for less than a mile but in the heat of the valley, his strength had all but sapped away.

Before him the channel of the gorge split and he had to choose which way to go. The passage to his left seemed the obvious choice. It was flatter and straighter than the other, which rose up a hill.

He glanced over his shoulder.

The mares of his pursuers were momentarily out of sight.

At once, he turned his steed to the right, thinking if he could clear the rise, he'd be hidden on the other side. With any luck, the Vipers would continue straight on, and he could then double-back and return to the village.

"Come on," he yelled, urging Mott up the slope.

The stallion snorted.

He was nearly done.

Dirk could feel the sweat on his neck dripping down over the reins.

"Forward boy," he said, leaning down and whispering into the horse's ear. "Just a few more yards and we'll be safe."

Mott forced himself up the slope, giving it everything he had. Once he had cleared the crest he teetered on his hooves and came to an involuntary stop.

He was completely spent.

Dirk quickly dismounted and led him over to the cliff face, where he could cool down in the shade.

"Well done, boy," he said, patting the horse's nose. "You saved us both."

Suddenly he heard a whinny to his left and turned his head to see Ermus and Varek ascending the slope.

"Did you think we're stupid," the fair-skinned Guildsman declared. "There were two paths and five of us."

Ermus smirked.

"Did it not occur to you we'd split up?"

Dirk stepped out into the light and drew his *Hunter's Bite*. The weapon's sharp edge gleamed brightly as it caught the rays of the sun.

"I'll not go quietly," Dirk warned, as Ermus and Varek climbed down from their saddles and strode forward.

"You're making a mistake," Varek said, drawing his blade.

"A big one," Ermus added, whose sword was already in his hand.

"We'll see, won't we?" Dirk replied.

The two men approached him cautiously, spreading apart so they could attack him from either side.

"This'll be a lot less painful if you let us take you," Varek laughed, tracing his blade through the air.

Dirk stepped back.

He knew the men would try to trap him against the wall. If that happened, he would surely be killed. His only hope was to keep them at bay and exploit any mistakes they made.

But it was easier said than done

If anyone were to make an error, it would more likely be him. He was the one moving backwards. All it would take would be for him to lose his footing and fall.

If that happened, it was over.

Dirk noticed Ermus chuckling as he edged in from the left.

He twisted his sword, and it caught the glare of the sun.

For a moment Dirk was blinded.

He stepped back and Varek lunged at him from the right. Dirk quickly raised his sword to parry, but before their swords had even touched, Ermus took a stab at him at him from the other side.

Thinking fast, Dirk jumped backward, avoiding both strikes.

"It's over for you," Varek growled. "You can't beat us both. Give it up, traitor."

"You're the traitor," Dirk replied. "You sacrificed your honour for blood and gold."

Varek smirked.

"I don't do this for gold," he laughed.

For blood then... Dirk thought.

Varek took another pace forward and Dirk quickly skipped to his left, which took him back to the centre of the riverbed.

Ermus then darted forward, sweeping his sword through the air towards Dirk's midriff. The serrated teeth of the weapon, which gave the *Hunter's Bite* its name, trapped the edge of Dirk's blade as he parried. The force of the blow carried the steel into his side, but the leather plates sewn into his tunic protected him from harm.

Varek then lunged in, thrusting his sword at Dirk's chest. With his arm pinned at his waist, he could do nothing but leap to his side and roll out of the way.

He heard a clatter as he spun over the hard rock, and as he planted his feet, he realised he'd dropped his weapon. Unarmed and outnumbered, Dirk could do nothing but back away.

"You're finished, coward," Ermus mocked. "You might as well get down on your knees and let us finish you off. We promise it won't hurt... Much."

Varek came forward once more but Dirk skipped backwards, out of harm's way. Out of the corner of his eye, he saw Ermus closing in on the left. Dirk mirrored the long-haired Guildsman's movements, believing that if he circled around them, he could trick them into crossing each other's paths.

Varek, however, sensed what he was doing, and responded by pacing backwards and then swinging round his partner's flank.

All of a sudden, Dirk found himself trapped between them with his back to the cliff.

With nowhere left to go, he could do nothing more but stand his ground as they boxed him in.

A sense of despair loomed over him.

This was it, he thought, *the place he would die...*

He wondered which of the two would deliver the fatal blow?

Would it be the arrogant Ermus, the longhaired Imperial, or Varek, the cruel northerner?

Not that it mattered...

Either way, he'd be dead, and his father's killer would escape justice.

In the end, it was Ermus who made the first move.

He came in from the left, his sword raised high in the air.

Dirk lifted his arm to parry, anticipating the pain that would soon follow....

But it never came.

Instead, Ermus seemed to freeze mid-strike, petrified like a statue.

His sword fell from his hands and he crumbled to the ground.

As he hit the floor, Dirk noticed the hilt of a dagger protruding from the socket of his left eye.

Dirk glanced to his right and saw Varek gazing up at the ridge above them, his face white with fear. A second later he turned tail and ran as fast as he could toward the horses.

Dirk stepped away from the slope and craned his neck upwards. Standing along the ridgeline were five Elven warriors, armed with bows. One of them pointed at Varek and the others shot arrows at him, but none of them found their mark and the Guildsman reached his steed unscathed. He then climbed up into his saddle then thundered away down the gorge.

Dirk looked up at his unlikely saviours.

"Stay where you are," one of them said.

He raised his hands and watched as they slid down the sloping walls of the canyon to meet him at the bottom.

All of them wore long hooded cloaks, which were dusky brown and perfectly matched the colour of the landscape.

Their leader came forward and removed her hood.

She was young, female and incredibly beautiful.

Her skin was fair, and her hair was long, straight and dark as night. Like her companions, it had been shaved around her ears to accentuate their pointed tips.

"What are you doing here?" she asked, as she plucked the dagger from the Ermus' eye.

Remembering his training, he answered with only his name and designation.

"I'm Dirk Vanslow," he replied. "A Guildsman."

"I can see that" she snorted. "But why are you here?"

He didn't respond.

She stood up and approached him with the bloodied knife.

Dirk bit his lip.

Any mention of the village could get him killed.

"Answer me," she spat.

"I'm only obliged to give you my name and rank," Dirk replied.

"I'm not interested in your name or rank," she said. "I want to know what you're doing here, trespassing in our lands?"

"These aren't your lands," Dirk replied. "They belong to the Empire."

"Not for long," she said.

Dirk kept his cool.

"We should just kill him and be done with it," one of her companions said.

"No," she declared. "We're not murderers."

"What then?" he snorted. "Let him go?"

She stepped forward and looked Dirk in the eye.

"We'll take him back to camp," she said. "If he won't talk to us, maybe he'll talk to Araxys."

Dirk's heart skipped at the mention of his name.

"You're the Swords of Sheenah..." he said.

"Yes," she replied. "And you are now our prisoner."

* * *

Dirk's hands were bound, and a hood was placed over his head. He was then taken to the top of the cliff where he heard the neighing of horses. His arms were seized, and he was lifted up onto one of the saddles, where the cords that tied his wrists were wrapped around the pommel.

The air beneath the hood was stifling.

"Do I really have to wear this?" Dirk asked.

"Yes," the She-Elf replied.

"But it's too hot," he complained. "I can hardly breathe."

"If you can talk, you can breathe," she replied sharply.

She issued an order to her troops and the train of horses moved out.

After an hour or so of riding, their canter slowed to a trot and he heard one of the riders sidling up beside him.

"Thirsty yet?" a voice said.

It was the She-Elf.

"Yes," Dirk replied.

He was parched.

His throat had never felt drier.

"I'll give you some water," she replied. "...If you answer my questions."

Dirk shook his head.

He wasn't ready to break.

Not yet, at least...

"There's no point being so stubborn," she said. "You'll end up talking anyway. Everyone does when they meet my father."

Dirk smirked beneath the hood.

"Then why bother speaking to you?"

He heard her hiss.

The words had struck a nerve.

Maybe she was keen to impress him?

"My father thinks I'm weak," she admitted. "...That I lack the strength to do this."

"And you think torturing me will prove otherwise?"

He heard her snort.

She leaned over to his saddle and lifted up the base of his hood. With her free hand, she held her skein up to his mouth.

The water felt like heaven to his lips, and he lapped up as much as he could.

"Better?" she asked.

"Yes," he replied.

"Well?" she said.

Dirk laughed.

"Normally the reward follows the bribe," he said.

She clicked her tongue at him.

"Call it a sweetener then," she quipped. "I'll give you the whole skein if you answer my questions."

Dirk thought about it.

He didn't know when he'd next be allowed to drink... or if at all.

"Fine," he said. "What do you want to know?"

"You can start by telling me why those men were trying to kill you."

Dirk sighed.

"Because I wouldn't follow their orders," he said.

"Why?" she asked.

Dirk shook his head.

He knew that if he mentioned Shafarr, she'd kill him on the spot.

"I can't say," he replied.

She grunted with frustration.

"Fine," she hissed. "It matters not. You've admitted you're a traitor. That's all I need to know."

"I'm not a traitor," Dirk declared.

"How so, if you defied them?"

"They betrayed themselves," he rasped.

"How?" she asked.

"By breaking their vows."

She laughed.

"Guildsmen have no respect for their vows," she chuckled.

"I do," Dirk replied.

She sniffed.

"Then you're the exception..."

"I could say the same for you," Dirk replied. "You could have killed me back there, but you didn't."

She laughed.

"You think we're savages, don't you?"

Dirk said nothing.

Everything he'd seen so far suggested they were.

"We're the Swords of Sheenah," she declared, proudly. "We serve the Goddess and fight with honour."

It was Dirk's turn to sniff.

"Tell that to the children you murdered in Victory Square."

"What?"

She sounded genuinely surprised.

"It happened last night," he added. "Ask your father about it. I'm sure he gave the order."

"Lies," she hissed.

"It's the truth," Dirk replied. "I was there. I saw it with my own eyes."

She huffed and seemed unable to respond.

He heard her spur her horse.

"The skein!" he shouted.

But she was already gone.

Dirk cursed his loose tongue.

As the sound of her horse grew fainter, he wondered why they were keeping the truth from her?

She'd told him her father thought she was weak.

But was she really too weak to handle the truth?

...Or just too idealistic to accept it?

79

Either way, her reaction was telling.

It wasn't something she'd wanted to hear...

* * *

They continued riding across the arid wasteland for several more hours. Every minute that passed, the more stifling his hood became, and Dirk felt himself wilting in the saddle.

He felt like he was going to faint.

A few more minutes and he would.

Just then one of the riders in the train called out and the horses slowed to a trot. He heard sounds up ahead, the clinking of cans and people talking.

It sounded like a camp.

As they got closer, he heard the footsteps of people running out to greet them.

"Who's that in the hood?" a voice said.

"A prisoner," one of the riders replied. "A Guildsman."

"Scum!" someone shouted.

"Roundear filth!" another one yelled.

Dirk tried to ignore them as best as he could.

The horses plodded into the camp and came to a stop.

He heard the riders around him dismount and a couple of them came over to his horse and untied the bonds fixing him to the pommel. They then coaxed him down from the saddle and took him inside a tent, where they made him sit with his back against a wooden stake that had been driven into the ground. His captors pulled his hands behind his back and clicked his wrists inside a set of iron manacles.

Finally, the She-Elf lifted his hood.

He gasped at the air.

"You'll stay here until the council are ready to see you," she said, lifting a skein of water to his lips.

He supped at the cool liquid furiously.

He'd never felt a thirst like it.

"That's enough," she spat, pulling the flask away from his

mouth.

She stood up then left with her comrades through the flap.

Dirk looked round.

The tent was small, stuffy and dark; the only source of light coming from a strong beam of sunlight, which shone through a tiny tear in the roof.

As far as prisons went, it was a horrible one.

But it could easily have been worse...

CHAPTER 8

Several hours passed by, and the light streaming through the hole in the roof of the tent began to fade. Within minutes, the temperature dropped considerably, and he found himself shivering on the spot.

He heard the sound of footsteps outside and the entrance flap was lifted. Three Elven warriors then entered the tent wearing the same dusky brown cloaks of his captors. They came forward, unlocked his manacles, and hauled him to his feet.

"Where are you taking me?" he asked.

The warriors didn't answer.

They seized his arms and led him outside.

The cold air stung his face.

He looked around and for the first time saw the camp.

It consisted of two rows of fifteen tents. They were dusty brown in colour and perfectly matched the shade of the surrounding desert.

The soldiers led him to the end of the row then turned right into the desert.

At once Dirk feared the worst.

In the back of his mind, he pictured Major Patz being pinned to the floor of the desert with his sword.

Would the same fate now befall him?

Then up ahead, he saw the light of a fire.

It was coming from a brazier that had been erected in the sand.

As he got closer, he saw that it had been fashioned into the shape of a spiral and resembled the obelisk in the village.

People were sitting in a semi-circle around it.

Elves.

Many looked old or middle-aged. Some wore the robes of priests; others were dressed in the same cloaks as his captors.

They all turned their heads as he approached and Dirk averted his gaze.

The guards brought him before the fire then sat him down and bound his hands and feet. They then stepped back, leaving him to the mercy of the stares.

Finally, someone spoke.

"What were you doing in our lands?"

Dirk recognised the voice.

He'd heard it in his dreams every night.

It was Araxys.

The man who'd murdered his father.

He lifted his head and looked the speaker in the eye.

He'd aged somewhat since that fateful day but the patch covering his eye was as unmistakable as his arrogant smile.

"Well?" he asked.

Dirk didn't reply.

He was too incensed to speak.

"My daughter, Marfine, said she caught you in the Shemali Gorge..." Araxys continued, gesturing to the She-Elf, who was sitting beside him. "She also said you refused to answer her questions?"

"It's my right," Dirk replied.

"Not here it isn't," Araxys sneered. "This is an Elven Council. You either speak to us or die. It's your choice."

He smiled wickedly.

Dirk needed to think fast.

If he didn't give the council something, he'd end up like the Major.

"Ok, I'll talk," he said. "But not about my mission..."

Araxys smirked and gestured to the guards, who came forward and seized him by the arms.

"Wait!" Dirk yelled, as he dragged him away. "I know about

the Firepowder."

Murmurs rippled through the council.

Araxys raised his hand and the guards checked their stride.

"What of it?" he asked.

"It's being moved," Dirk replied. "It's not being kept where you think it is."

"And you know its location?"

"Yes."

The Rebel Leader smiled.

"I suppose you're willing to tell us in exchange for your life?"

Dirk nodded.

Araxys shook his head.

"Do you think we're stupid, boy?" he said. "If we let you go, you'll go running to the Guild."

"No," Dirk replied. "They want to kill me. I betrayed them."

"It's true," Marfine yelled. "They were trying to kill him. I saw it."

"Why?" Araxys asked.

Dirk sighed and shook his head.

"Fine," he replied. "Tell your story to the crows."

"Wait," Marfine said. "This is Sheenahic council."

Araxys sniffed but Dirk noticed consternation in the crowd.

Her words were greeted with nods from the council.

"Our cause is one that serves the Goddess," she declared. "So we must settle his fate in accordance with her law."

The council murmured with approval.

Even the Elves who had seemed to be in agreement with Araxys were now bobbing their heads.

"Fine," Araxys sighed, responding to the change of mood. "Let's do this the Sheenahic way...

He turned to the crowd.

"Those in favour of killing him..." he said.

Dirk glanced around the circle and saw a number of arms

being raised.

It was a clear majority.

Araxys smiled.

He'd won.

"The council has spoken," he declared. "Take him away."

"You're making a mistake," Dirk yelled.

Araxys smirked, and the soldiers who were holding his arms marched him way from the brazier.

Suddenly, a rider appeared on the horizon.

He was coming from the direction of the camp.

The Elves in the council stood up and watched him as he approached.

"Who is it?" someone said.

"Ergule," someone answered. "It's Ergule."

The horse trotted forward into the firelight and Dirk looked up at the rider.

It was an old man.

His faced seemed familiar.

It was the elder from the village.

He reined in his horse and dismounted.

Araxys stepped forward.

"Wise one," he said reverently. "What are you doing here?"

"I came from Shemali," the old man replied. "Something terrible has happened."

One of the guards took the bit of his horse as he stepped forward.

"What happened?" Araxys asked.

"The village was attacked," he replied. Many were killed."

There was a collective gasp from the council.

Dirk heard names being called.

They must have had relatives there.

"Who did this?" Araxys asked.

"The Guild," the elder replied gravely.

The Rebel Leader turned scowled at Dirk.

"Murderous scum," he rasped. "No wonder you wouldn't talk."

He drew the dagger from his belt.

"For this outrage, I'll kill you myself..."

He stepped forward and with his knife, but the old man stayed his hand.

"No," he said, looking at Dirk. "This one had nothing to do with it."

"But he's one of them," someone in the crowd retorted.

The elder shook his head.

"He tried to save us," he said. "He turned against his comrades to stop the bloodshed... If it wasn't for him, they'd have killed us all."

Marfine stood up, open-jawed.

Araxys stepped forward and looked him in the eye.

"Is this true?" he asked.

Dirk met his gaze and nodded.

"Why?"

"Because he's a man of honour," Marfine replied.

Araxys snorted and smiled snobbishly.

"The Guild have no honour..." he sneered.

His words were stated as a fact.

Many in the crowd seemed to agree.

"Kill him," Araxys said.

"No," someone shouted. "Recast the vote."

At least half the crowd murmured in agreement.

"The decision has already been made," he snapped.

"No it hasn't," Marfine replied. "Only one side was heard."

Araxys glared at her.

"Fine," he said.

He turned to face the council.

"Those in favour of letting him live?"

Many hands were raised.

It was clear some of the council had changed their minds.

Dirk's eyes drifted to Marfine.

She responded with a warm smile.

* * *

Once the council had dispersed, Dirk was untied and taken back to the camp by the guards. As they marched him back towards his tent, Marfine joined them.

"Was it true?" she asked, sidling up beside him.

"Was what true?" Dirk replied.

"What you did at Shafarr?" she said. "Did you really save those people?"

"I tried," he replied.

She looked confused.

"Why? They were Elves. They meant nothing to you."

"They were innocent," Dirk said. "And what happened there was wrong."

"You really are a man of honour."

"I did my duty," Dirk replied. "The same way you did."

She smiled.

When they reached his tent the soldiers ushered him inside and secured him to the stake.

"What's wrong?" Marfine asked, as his hands were clicked inside the iron manacles. "Are you not happy that the council let you live?"

Dirk glanced over his shoulder at his cuffed wrists.

"I'd be happier if I didn't have to wear these," he replied. "There's no way I can sleep like this."

She gestured to one of the warriors, who unlocked his cuffs.

He brought his hands in front of him.

"Aren't you worried I'll escape?" he asked.

"Where to?" she laughed. "We're in the middle of the desert, miles from any town. Whichever way you ran, you'd freeze to death by morning."

Dirk smirked.

"Still," he replied. "That's awfully trusting of you."

Marfine placed her hands on her hips.

"Don't make me regret it," she said. "Or I'll kill you myself."

She handed him her skein, then turned on her heels and

left the tent.

Dirk smiled and leant back against the stake.

He'd been lucky tonight.

Very lucky...

The hands of fate had worked in his favour.

In a matter of seconds, he'd gone from being a man condemned to one who had the freedom of his enemy's castle.

His thoughts turned to the prayer he'd said in the Silent Valley.

Had V'Loire heard his plea?

Was he helping him?

Chance alone could not have put him here, in the home of his enemy, unwatched and untethered?

Surely it was a sign...

He waited until the camp grew quiet then made his way over to the entrance.

Peeking outside, he saw no one around.

Everyone, it seemed, had gone to sleep.

He quietly lifted the flap, stepped outside, then made his way to the rear of his tent and began creeping along the row.

Araxys was here somewhere.

And he wouldn't stop until he found him.

He crouched down beside the neighbouring tent and put his ear to the canvass. Inside, someone was snoring. The tone was low, male and indistinct, but when the dreamer began talking in his sleep, Dirk knew it wasn't his man.

He moved onto the next.

Listening outside, he heard nothing.

As he started creeping up to the third, he suddenly heard voices talking within another tent further up. Ducking low, he carefully made his way towards it and leant in to listen.

A woman was speaking.

He recognised the voice.

It belonged to Marfine.

She was talking about a planned kidnapping of the Ghisian Governor during his next trip to Royal Kronnig. She sounded angry that the details had not been shared with her.

A male Elf replied.

It was Araxys.

"You know the nature of these things," he told her. "The details must be kept secret."

"From me?" Marfine replied. "Your own daughter? Don't you trust me?"

"I trust you completely, my dear," Araxys replied.

"Then why wasn't I told?"

Araxys sighed.

"Let's speak of this tomorrow," he said, avoiding the answer.

"Why tomorrow?" she replied. "Why not now?"

"Because it's late," he replied firmly. "...And we both need rest."

"Don't treat me like a child," she said. "I know you're hiding something from me. What is it?"

"Patience, my child," Araxys said. "You'll know everything in good time."

"Like what happened in Victory Square?"

"What of it?" he said.

"I heard that innocent people were killed."

There was a rasp to her voice.

She was clearly upset.

"Who told you that?" he asked. "The Guildsman?"

"So what if he did?" she replied. "Is it true?"

"No," Araxys replied.

"Don't lie to me," she said. "You promised my mother on her deathbed that we would never dishonour the Goddess."

"And I've kept that promise," Araxys lied. "Every day."

"*On Sheenah's Truth*," she declared, patting her chest.

"*On Sheenah's Truth*," he repeated.

Marfine let out a sigh of acceptance.

"Now get some sleep, child. We set off early tomorrow."

"Good night father."

The flap of the tent lifted.

He ducked down low as she came out and made her way along the row to her quarters... Leaving Araxys all alone.

Dirk stood up gingerly then quietly made his way around the side of the tent towards the entrance.

Just then, he saw the shadow of a figure walking between the rows.

It was a guard.

"Who's that?" he called out.

Dirk cursed his bad luck.

V 'Loire, it seemed, had forsaken him.

He immediately backed up and crouched down behind the tent.

The guard turned and began walking down the side of the tent.

Another pace and he would see him.

Thinking fast, Dirk launched himself over the crest of the dune behind him. The sand was as fine as dust and he made no sound as he slid to the bottom.

Turning his ear upwards, he heard the clinking of the guard's armour as he approached the rear of the tent.

"Show yourself," the man ordered.

Dirk remained perfectly still.

The man above him didn't move.

But if he were to take a single step forward, he would see him below.

Dirk froze and held his breath, trying to stay as silent as possible.

The Guard wasn't going away.

Dirk then noticed something moving in the moonlight, a small creature scurrying towards him across the freezing dust.

It was a *Sand Hare*.

He remembered them from when he a boy.

They were curious animals, known for their stupidity. It stopped just short of his feet and looked up at him.

Suddenly, he had an idea.

Lifting his hand, he coaxed it toward him by rubbing his

thumb against his forefinger. The Sand Hare stopped and looked to the sound. It then tilted its head and hopped forward.

In a flash, Dirk scooped it up in his palm and threw it across the dune to his left.

The creature yelped as it landed, and he heard the Guard step forward to look. At once, Dirk spun away to his right and snuck away along the dune.

Once he was out of sight, he climbed back up the dune and returned to his tent, where he lay down on the floor and closed his eyes.

Araxys had escaped him tonight but there would no doubt be other chances.

All he needed to do was bide his time...

* * *

He woke up the next morning to the sounds of activity within the camp. Sitting up from the floor, he rubbed the salt from his eyes and drank from his skein.

He then put on his clothes and boots then stepped outside to find the camp in a state of organised disarray. Many of the soldiers were taking down their tents and loading them onto a large cart, which had been parked in the centre of the row.

To his left, he saw Marfine with Araxys and a number of her men. They were kneeling together on the ground and looked to be in prayer.

He took another sip from the flask and wandered over, watching them as they raised their arms to the sky before bowing down low and touching the earth with their fingertips.

As he got closer, he heard them chanting.

It was a language that seemed both familiar and not. He wondered which tongue they were speaking, given that the common language of Ethren was *Prutch*?

Marfine noticed him as he approached. She glanced at her father, who replied with a nod, and she left the group and came over.

"What's wrong?" she asked.

"Nothing," Dirk replied. "It's just that I've never seen Elves praying before."

"Humans do not pray to V'Loire?" she said.

"We do," he replied. "Once in the morning and twice at night."

She smiled.

"We only pray when we need assistance," she replied.

"Does it work?" he asked.

"Always," she replied.

"So what's going on?" he asked, glancing around the camp. "Are we moving?"

"They are," Marfine replied. "But you're coming with us."

"Where?" Dirk asked.

"Ghis," she said. "You're going to tell us where the Firepowder is."

Dirk smirked.

"Yes," he said. "But I didn't think I'd be coming along..."

"Why not?" she replied. "This way, if you're telling us lies we won't need to come all the way back here to kill you."

He laughed.

"You think I'd lie to you?"

"Would you?"

She gave him a cursory look.

Had she changed her mind about him?

Or was she still conflicted?

It was hard to tell.

He looked into her eyes.

"I guess you'll just have to trust me," he replied.

CHAPTER 9

They rode west through the desert all morning, stopping only to water the horses. There were six of them in all, Araxys, Marfine, and three other warriors named Dustyn, Tressyn, and Olojeon, the Elf who'd recently visited Ruyven's Rumhouse.

By the late afternoon they'd sighted the city walls and Araxys had ordered them to stop in a dry Wadi about half a mile from town, where they would wait until nightfall. Once they'd tethered the horses, Dustyn opened his saddlebags and began handing out food and water to the group.

They all then sat with their backs against the Wadi's sloping sides and waited for the sun to set.

As Dirk settled down on his haunches, a number of them produced books that had been concealed beneath their cloaks. They were copies of the She'En, the Elven equivalent of the Testament.

When Marfine saw the curious look on his face, she brought over her copy and handed it to him.

"Have you ever read our scriptures?" she asked.

He took the tome from her and looked at the cover, which was elaborately decorated in gold print.

"No," he said. "Sheenah is the Elven God."

"Sheenah is everyone's God," she replied. "Whom do you think Humans followed before V'Loire?"

He opened up the pages and began reading.

The sentences were written in Middle Prutch, but he had no trouble translating, as he'd studied the language at Guildschool.

"I recognise this," he said, after reading the first verse. "It's the story of the creation."

He finished the first paragraph and was stunned to find that it was near identical to the writings of the Testament.

"I learned this as a child."

Tressyn laughed.

"The world didn't start with V'Loire..." he chuckled.

Marfine gave him an angry look.

"Here," she said to Dirk. "Take it."

"Thank you," he said.

She left him be and he continued to study the Elven text as the sun slowly fell beyond the Western horizon.

He liked the way it was written.

Unlike the Testament, which was clunky and at times bumbling, the She'En possessed a beautiful simplicity, which gave its stories a ring of truth.

However, there were some things he didn't understand.

The passages on Morality, for example were hugely different from the V'Loire dogma. According to the Testament, justice was akin to revenge, but here the message was different...

Here, it wasn't described as a proscription, but as a feeling - 'that which calmed the heart'.

He wondered what it meant.

It seemed confusing, almost contradictory.

Was it saying that people shouldn't be punished at all?

That criminals should be forgiven and let go?

It didn't make any sense.

Why shouldn't they be punished?

Why shouldn't they get what they deserved?

An eye-for-an-eye, a tooth-for-a-tooth...

What could be fairer than that?

Yet despites his misgivings, there was something oddly compelling about it.

He turned to Marfine and asked her if she could explain what the passage meant but she smiled and shook her head.

"The words of the Goddess are sometimes veiled," she replied. "But everything make sense in time."

"What if it never does?" Dirk replied.

"It always does," Tressyn said. *"The Truth will always prevail."*

"The Truth will always prevail," Dustyn repeated.

Dirk nodded, reverently.

He closed the book and offered it to Marfine.

"Keep it," she said, holding up her hand.

"Are you sure?" he replied.

She bobbed her head.

"Don't lose it," Dustyn warned.

"Yes," Marfine added. "If you keep it safe, it'll keep *you* safe."

He gave her a nod of thanks then slid the tome beneath his tunic.

* * *

Several hours later, once the moon had risen and was shining brightly in sky, Araxys climbed the sides of the Wadi and peered out over the edge.

"Ok," he said. "Time to go."

Dirk looked at Marfine, who gestured for him to follow the line of warriors as they vaulted the sides of the crevasse and began hiking across the open ground towards the city.

During his initial tour of Ghis, Varek had informed him that the City Guard manned the walls at all times and were always watching out for potential threats. As they got closer to the fortifications, Dirk saw a number of soldiers standing amongst the battlements, armed with bows and spears.

He turned to Marfine, who was running alongside him.

"What if they see us?" he asked.

"Don't worry," she replied. "It's all taken care of."

As if on cue, the sentries on top of the walls walked along the run and disappeared into the towers.

It was clear they had been bribed.

They continued forward and stopped at the bottom of a

section of wall just west of the Southern Gate.

"What do we do now?" Dirk asked.

Marfine smiled and pointed upwards.

Dirk craned his neck and looked up the walls.

At the top he saw a length of rope being lowered from between the battlements. As it dropped down amongst them Dustyn seized it and began climbing up. The others watched from the bottom as he scaled the walls and reached the top. Once he'd swung over his legs, he waved a signal to the group below.

"It's clear," Araxys said. "Go."

Marfine then took the line and began their ascent.

Araxys and Tressyn followed her.

Once they were at the top, Olojeon handed the rope to Dirk and ordered him to climb.

He took the line in his hands and began pulling himself up.

Being broader than the rest of them, it took him longer to ascend, and by the time he'd reached the top, he was out of breath.

Planting his feet upon the run, he glanced up and saw the tower of the citadel looming above him. It was silhouetted in the moonlight and cast a dark shadow upon them, hiding them from view.

He looked to his right, and saw the others pulling on the rope. Moments later, the muscular form of Olojeon appeared at the top. They helped him over the wall then lowered the rope down the other side.

Dirk peered over the edge of the run. Below them was a narrow alley, which lay behind a row of houses.

"Let's go," Marfine said, as she swung over the side and began rappelling down.

When she reached the bottom, she waved up and Araxys took the line and shimmied down after her. Tressyn and Dustyn then followed, before Olojeon handed the rope to Dirk.

It was a clear sign he wasn't trusted.

He sat down on the run, took hold of the rope and dropped

over the side, lowering himself slowly, hand-under-hand, until he reached the bottom. Olojeon then slid down after him.

Once they were all together, Araxys began leading them through the alley towards the river, hugging the line of the city walls.

Because it was so late, the majority of the Ghisians were tucked up in their beds, and they encountered few people on the way, mostly drunks, who paid them no attention as they darted between the shadows.

When they reached the water's edge, they turned west and made their way along the shore toward the harbour, where they stopped beneath the bridge that crossed the Rhund into Victory Square.

Propped up against the inside stanchion was a large rowing boat with two sets of oars. Dustyn and Tressyn approached it and tipped it onto its side. As they began dragging it into the water, Dirk felt a hand upon his shoulder.

He turned his head.

It was Araxys.

"Time for you to deliver on your end of the deal," he muttered grimly. "Where are they keeping the Firepowder?"

"The south-side warehouse," Dirk replied.

Olojeon sniffed.

"The ship's manifest said it was to be taken to the north."

"It was," Dirk said. "But they knew you were coming so they set a trap."

"How do you know this?" the Elf asked.

"One of my former comrades told me," he said.

"Was that before or after you turned traitor?" Olojeon sneered.

Dirk smirked.

"Before," he replied passively.

Araxys looked into Dirk's eyes.

"You'd better not be lying to us," he said.

"I'm not," Dirk replied.

The Rebel Leader smiled.

"Ok," he said. "But if it turns out you're leading us into an ambush..."

"...I'll kill you," Marfine finished.

Araxys glanced at his daughter and nodded.

For the first time, he looked impressed.

He ordered Tressyn and Dustyn to row the boat out to the south-side jetty, then led the rest of the group along the shoreline to the Southern Depots.

Under the cover of darkness, they dashed across the harbourside before making their way into the alley that separated the Warehouse from the row of Taverns. Once there, Olojeon jimmied open the side-door.

Araxys looked at Dirk.

"You first," he said.

Dirk hesitated.

It occurred to him that the Guild might have changed plans after what had happened at Shafarr.

Maybe they had anticipated that after he was captured, he'd use his knowledge of the raid against them, so had sent the Firepowder somewhere else?

Maybe they were waiting inside right now, ready to ambush them as they entered.

Regardless, Dirk had no choice.

With a grimace, he crossed the threshold.

To his relief he found the warehouse was empty and unguarded.

"It's clear," he said, beckoning the others to enter.

Marfine, Olojeon and Araxys stepped inside.

The four of them then began looking around for the shipment and Marfine soon found it beneath a sheet against the far wall.

"Check it," Araxys ordered, and Olojeon jabbed the side of the barrels with his dagger. When he removed his blade, a stream of black powder poured from the hole. It was thick like unground pepper and smelled of sulphur.

"It's good," the Elf said, as he plugged the holed with a

piece of fabric.

"Good," Araxys replied. "Let's get out of here."

Marfine jogged over to the main doors and began picking the lock, while Dirk and Olojeon turned the barrel on its side and began rolling it toward her.

When the latch clicked, Araxys swung open the large front doors and they rolled the cask out, first down the ramp, and then along the harbourside to the pontoon.

Waiting at the end of the jetty were Dustyn and Tressyn in the rowing boat. The two Elves waved to them as they turned the barrel onto the jetty and pushed it to the mooring.

"Quickly," Araxys said. "Get it on board."

With a mighty heave, Dirk and Olojeon lifted the barrel and lowered it down onto the hull, the punt bobbing in the water as it took the weight.

As he helped shift it into position, Dirk at once realised there was only space aboard for five of them.

He turned and looked at Araxys.

The Rebel Leader nodded at Olojeon, who then seized Dirk by the arms.

"What's going on?" Marfine exclaimed.

"We're casting off the dead weight," her father replied.

Olojeon pulled out his knife.

"No," Marfine yelled. "We made a deal!"

Araxys smiled.

"I'm changing the terms," he replied.

"You can't," she said. "You promised..."

"A promise made to a Guildsman is no promise at all."

"But he helped us," Marfine pleaded. "If not for him we'd have all been caught."

"Helped us?" he laughed. "He's a spy."

"No, he's not."

"If that's the case..." Araxys said. "What was he doing sneaking around the camp last night?"

Marfine looked at Dirk with aching eyes.

"Is it true?" she asked.

Dirk smiled apologetically.

Araxys looked him in the eye.

"What were you looking for?" he asked.

There was no point keeping up the pretence.

"You," Dirk replied.

"Why?" Araxys asked.

"Revenge."

Araxys laughed.

"For what?" he chuckled. "I don't even know you."

"Oh, but you do..." Dirk replied. "Six years ago, you attacked a cart leaving Ghis. I was on that cart with my father. You killed him, stole our coin, and left me for dead."

"Is this true?" Marfine asked, shocked.

"No," Araxys snapped. "He's lying."

Olojeon raised his blade but Marfine stayed his hand.

"No," she said. "Let me do it."

Araxys raised an eyebrow.

"I told him that if he betrayed us, I'd kill him myself."

"Very well," Araxys said.

Olojeon handed her the knife.

She looked Dirk in the eye.

"You made me trust you," she said...then thrust the blade into his chest.

Olojeon let go of his arms and he fell backwards from the jetty into the water below. He looked up through the murk and as the current carried him downstream the silvery silhouettes of the three Elves disappeared from view.

For a moment, he wondered why he couldn't feel any pain.

The knife had penetrated his tunic and the point of the blade had been over his heart. But as he drifted through the water, he could not feel the steel touching his flesh...

Maybe death was painless, he thought to himself?

He reached up to his chest and found the dagger's hilt.

It was still there, embedded.

The river pushed him westwards and as he drifted to the side of its banks, his body washed up on the silt of the shore.

100

Rolling over onto his knees, he lifted himself up, gasping at the air as he broke the surface. He looked down at the knife. It was stuck tight and its blade sparkled in the moonlight.

He got to his feet up and pulled at the handle.

Something tugged at his chest, and at once he realised what had happened.

The steel of the knife had pierced the book Marfine had given him in the Wadi. He undid the buttons of his tunic and pulled it out. The blade had sunk deep within the pages but not so far as to reach his chest. Had Marfine stabbed him there on purpose? She'd seen him place the book there, and must have felt the point strike it when she'd thrust her dagger into him...

She'd saved his life.

But why...?

He collapsed down onto the beach and caught his breath as the first rays of dawn appeared over the eastern sky.

He gathered his thoughts and pondered his next move.

Though he'd escaped death, his situation hadn't improved.

In truth, it had worsened.

He was no closer to avenging his father. Araxys had escaped, unscathed, and without the Guild's help, it was unlikely he'd ever find him again.

He also couldn't return to the Guildhouse, as the Vipers had probably issued a warrant for his arrest. If he presented himself at any Guild in Ethren, he'd be seized and charged, and without the evidence to clear his name, it was unlikely he'd be exonerated.

Fleeing was not an option either.

Given what had happened, the Guild would hunt him down wherever he went, and even if he managed to evade capture, he would eventually die knowing his father's killer had escaped justice...

At once he felt alone, isolated and lost.

There seemed to be no way out.

Then suddenly, he had an idea...

CHAPTER 10

Dirk opened the door of the Rumhouse and walked inside. A number of grizzled sailors turned their heads and looked at him. He recognised several of them from his first visit. Many of them looked as if they'd not moved from their seats.

"Where's Ruyven?" he asked, whilst standing in the doorway, the water from his clothes dripping onto the floorboards.

"Are you alone?" one of the sailors asked.

Dirk nodded.

The sailor stood up.

"Then I suggest you leave," the man said.

His words were echoed by the rum-bellies surrounding him. Beneath the tables, Dirk noticed that several of them had placed their hands on the hilts of their daggers.

"I don't want any trouble," Dirk said. "I just want to see the owner."

"You left him in a bad state last time you were here," the first sailor said.

He stood up and stepped forward into the light. Dirk saw that he was wearing a battered blue and white tunic embroidered with an image of a golden Kingfisher, which were the colours and national symbol of Hessell. Judging by the look of him, Dirk surmised that he was a former Marine who had retired in Ghis after serving in the navy.

"I'm not here to hurt him," he said. "I need his help."

A man at the back laughed.

"And why would he want to help you after what you did?"

"It wasn't me," Dirk protested. "It was Varek."

"You wear the same tunic," the first man noted. "Why

should we believe you're any different?"

"Listen," he said, holding up his hands. "I just need to talk to Ruyven."

"Talk to us first," a man to his right chimed.

Dirk glanced over and saw him stand.

This one was considerably younger and taller than his friend. His head was bald and covered with a bandana, and his forearms were huge and awash in tattoos.

The man stepped forward and Dirk retreated back a pace.

"I'm a Guildsman," he warned. "If anything happens to me, they'll be consequences."

"We don't care," the bald-headed man spat. "You hurt our mate."

He suddenly came forward and threw a punch at Dirk's face. Instinctively, he ducked then dodged to the side. The older man then lunged forward and seized him by the collar.

Dirk twisted away but ended up being sucker-punched in the ribs by the younger man. The force of the blow winded him and he gasped. The older man then grabbed his arms and pinned behind his shoulders.

"Hit him," the Marine yelled, as Dirk wrestled to break free.

The big man smiled and swung one of his meat hooks at Dirk's face. It struck him squarely in the jaw.

For a moment, he lost consciousness.

When he opened his eyes, he found himself on the floor, looking up at the men as they aimed kicks at his legs and chest.

"Stop!" Dirk yelled. "I don't want to fight you!"

"Too late for that," the older man snorted.

He launched a boot at his face, but Dirk quickly rolled away and avoided being struck.

The big man then leapt upon him, and he felt the weight of the man's knee pushing down on his chest. He tried to move his arms, but the brute shifted his bulk upwards, trapping his shoulders.

At once, he was vulnerable and undefended.

The man raised his fist.

"Don't!" a voice called from across the room.

Dirk tilted his head and saw the figure of Ruyven standing at the bar. His face was covered in bruises and he was walking with the aid of a stick.

"Leave him alone," the Elf said.

The big man gave him a cursory look then rose to his feet.

"If we let him go, they'll all come for you," he warned.

The Elf's eyes drifted to the floor.

"I know," he said, "But I can't let you kill him."

The Ex-Marine huffed.

"You're making a mistake," he warned.

"Then on my head be it," Ruyven answered.

Dirk saw sadness in his eyes. The man was thinking about his son and what might happen if word of this got out.

The big man stepped back, and Dirk stood up.

Ruyven then beckoned him forward and led him into the back room, where he poured him a measure of rum from one of the barrels.

"I'm truly sorry for what happened just now," he said. "What can I do to stop you from telling your friends?"

Dirk sipped from the glass.

The rum was strong and burned his throat as he swallowed, but as soon as he overcame the intense aftertaste, he felt his body relax as the spirit took effect.

"You can help me," Dirk replied.

"Help you?" Ruyven responded. "How?"

Dirk glanced around the barrels in the room then fixed his eyes on one that bore an import stamp from Gerwald.

"When's your next shipment of *Einhof Sweet*?" he asked.

"Tomorrow," Ruyven answered.

"Can you give the Captain a letter and ask him to take it to the Guildhouse on his return?"

Ruyven looked at him, confused.

"I need to send word the Guild Corps," Dirk continued. "I want to expose what's happening here; the corruption, the torture, the murder...."

"Why?" the Elf asked.

"Because it's the right thing to do."

Ruyven sighed sorrowfully.

"As much as I want these butchers to pay, I can't take the risk," he said. "If they inspect the ship before it sets sail, they'll trace the letter here then come for me."

"Please," Dirk pleaded. "You're the only person in this city I trust."

"Why don't you send a letter by courier instead?" Ruyven offered.

Dirk shook his head.

"The Guild know about me," he said. "They'll be watching the post, intercepting all riders heading for Einhof..."

Ruyven blew out his cheeks.

"You're asking a lot of me," he replied. "It's not only my life I'm risking but my son's too."

"I know," Dirk said, placing a comforting hand on the man's shoulder. "But if you want this to end, this is the only way."

It was clear Ruyven wanted to help but was fearful of what would happen, should the plan fail.

He let out a long sigh.

"When I left prison," he began, "I promised myself a new start."

He turned and gazed at the barrels of rum behind him.

"For the sake of my son," he continued. "I swore I'd never fight again..."

His fingers caressed one of the holes that had been made by Varek's dagger and his eyes dropped to the floor.

"...But I've been fighting each day ever since."

He glanced up.

"Maybe it's time I took a stand?" he said.

"Then you'll help me?" Dirk asked.

Ruyven looked him in the eye and nodded.

CHAPTER 11

Dirk steeled himself as he approached the Citadel. Its whitewashed towers rose a hundred feet in the air above him, casting a dark shadow across the road.

He took a breath as he stepped up to the doors, where two Guardsmen barred his way by crossing their halberds.

"What do you want?" one of them asked.

"I'm Dirk Vanslow," he replied. "There's a warrant on my head. I've come to turn myself in."

The guards gave him a curious look, then took him inside where they ushered him down a set of stairs to the jail. A fat guardsman met them at the bottom. He took Dirk's details then led him to his cell.

"Remember to inform the Guild Corps I'm here," he said, as the man closed the door plunging him into darkness.

Dirk looked around the room.

The only light came from a narrow slit that had been cut into the wall above the bed. The air was hot and smelled of sweat and death.

He went over to the bunk and sat down upon it.

Several hours later, he heard footsteps approaching outside and the turning of the key in the lock. Dirk got to his feet as the door swung open and Bakker and Mu'Ungo entered the room.

The Guildsergeant gestured to the Gaoler to leave them, and the man stepped outside and locked the door.

Before Dirk could utter a word, the Guildsergeant hit him across the face. The blow sent Dirk tumbling against the wall, where he hit his head and dropped to the floor.

"Did you really think this would work?" Bakker sneered. "Did you forget we own this city?"

"I claim my right to a trial," Dirk replied. "I demand to see the Guild Corps."

Bakker laughed.

"They can't help you here," he chuckled. "Your fate is in our hands now."

Dirk got to his feet and wiped the blood from his mouth.

"You don't have the authority to try me," he said.

"Who said anything about a trial?" the Guildsergeant replied. "We're going to take you out into the desert and bury you up to your head in the sand."

"You can't do that," Dirk replied.

Bakker smiled cruelly.

"This is Ghis," he replied. "I can do whatever I want."

He gestured to the Kulaanian, who reached for the set of manacles at his belt.

"Bind him," Bakker said.

Dirk stepped back, raising his hands.

"Wait," he said. "I can get you the Rebels."

"Rubbish," Bakker snorted. "They make camp in the desert. They're never in one place more than a night."

He gestured to Mu'Ungo, who paced forward.

Dirk backed up against the wall.

"I know what they're planning," he said. "You can set an trap."

Bakker held up his hand and the Kulaanian checked his stride.

"Go on," Bakker said.

"They're going after the Governor," Dirk said. "They're going to ambush his coach on his way to Kronnig."

"Be more specific," Bakker said. "Where?"

"I'll tell you," Dirk replied. "But I want something in return."

The Guildsergeant sniffed through his nose.

"Your freedom?" he laughed. "No chance."

"That's not what I want," Dirk replied.

"Then what do you want?"

Dirk held his gaze.

"Araxys," he replied.

"Why?" Bakker asked, raising an eyebrow.

"Because he killed my father."

The cruel smile disappeared from Bakker's face, and he gestured for Mu'Ungo to back off.

"I understand this need in you," he said, his words laced with sadness. "But be that as it may, I can't allow you to live."

"I don't care about living," Dirk continued. "I just want revenge..."

CHAPTER 12

The sun burned Dirk's back as he lay flat on the edge of the ridge. Bakker, Mu'Ungo and Varek were beside him. Peering over the cliff face, he watched as the coach carrying Count Lucas of Hellenburg, the Governor of Ghis, trundled through the Silent Valley.

It was strange to know his quest would end where it had started.

The Governor's carriage was travelling unescorted, as per his preference. Dirk had been told the man was young, aloof and arrogant, and like many of the Imperial family, believed himself to be so loved by the populace that he would never be a target for dissenters. The City Guard however, had adopted a more cautious approach, and had insisted that he travel with some form of protection. After much bickering, they'd reached a compromise and the Governor agreed to have armoured plates fitted to his carriage.

Dirk watched as the heavy coach trundled through the valley below, pulled by four northern stallions and driven by a coachman who was wearing full plate. Sitting on the bench alongside him were two crossbowmen wearing thick mail shirts.

"Where are the Rebels?" Bakker sneered, "You said they'd be here."

"They'll be here," Dirk replied.

But in his heart, he was less than sure.

Maybe their plans had changed, or it had never been their plan at all? All Dirk had to go on was what he'd heard outside Araxys' tent. For all he knew, it could have been nothing more than talk…

The prospect of that worried him.

If the *Swords* didn't show, his plan would go up in smoke.

And he would be left at the mercy of Bakker and his goons.

Come on, he thought, as the carriage rumbled along. *Show yourselves.*

Varek grunted with frustration.

"This is Orc shit," he snorted, "He lied to us."

He drew the dagger from his belt and held the blade beneath Dirk's chin.

"You're going to wish I'd have killed you in the gorge."

All of a sudden, a loud yell rang out from beyond the opposite ridge.

Varek sneered and withdrew the knife.

Dirk turned his head toward the sound as six Elven riders appeared on the cliff top. Araxys was among them, his distinctive eye-patch glowing in the midday sun.

So was Marfine.

The Guildsman remained still as the Elves descended the slope and thundered toward the carriage. Two of them drew short bows from their shoulders and loosed arrows at the crossbowmen sitting alongside the rider. Their steel tipped bolts pierced the mail of the men's hauberks and their bodies fell lifelessly from the seat. Seeing this, the driver panicked, and roared at the horses to go faster.

In response, Marfine spurred her mount to the front of the line, where she reached out her hand and took the leading stallion by the bit. The beast grunted then checked its stride. This imbalanced the train, splitting the leather straps that linked the horses to the pole. Seconds later the steeds on the left of the train broke free, and the central beam dipped toward the ground. It bit into the earth, and with a grinding screech the carriage came to a sudden halt, flinging the driver from his seat.

A thick cloud of dust was thrown up into the air, shrouding the scene with a light brown fog.

As the dust settled, Dirk witnessed the Elves climbing

down from their saddles. Among them, he saw the strident figure of Olojeon, who approached the stricken carriage, with a small parcel. He attached it to the armoured door and lit the short fuse that trailed from its bottom. He then ran away and ducked behind the rear wheel before the Firepowder inside it exploded, tearing a hole in the coach's side.

The Elves cheered triumphantly then advanced toward the smoking wreckage.

"Make ready," Bakker whispered beside him.

The men to his left and right drew their swords.

Dirk fixed his eyes on the carriage.

Olojeon was first to the door.

He climbed up onto the rig and peered inside.

A cry rang out.

The Elves behind him froze.

Olojeon's arms dropped to his sides, and his body fell backwards from the coach. As his body hit the earth, Dirk saw that his chest was covered in blood.

Marfine screamed.

"Now!" Bakker yelled.

The Guildsmen stood up, and with a ferocious roar, began sliding down the sides of the cliff towards the Elves.

Dirk swung his legs over the side and followed them, keeping his eyes on the carriage as he reached the bottom. A figure emerged from inside the smouldering wreck. It was Kort. He was smiling and holding a bloodied dagger.

The Viper's plan had worked perfectly.

The Elves had fallen for their ruse, hook, line and sinker.

"It's a trap!" Araxys yelled, as he realised what had happened. "Retreat!"

But it was too late.

The Guildsmen were already upon them.

To his right, Dirk saw Mu'Ungo engage the nearest Rebel. The Elven warrior barely had time to raise his sword as the huge Kulaanian barged him to the floor then ran him through with his *Hunter's Bite*.

Straight ahead, he saw Bakker taking on two warriors at once, whirling his blade like a man possessed.

To his left, he saw Varek charging towards an Elf armed with a shortbow. The Rebel fired a bolt at him, which pierced his shoulder. Ignoring the wound, Varek crashed into the Elf's midriff, bringing him down.

At once, Dirk noticed Araxys behind them. He was sneaking away, climbing up onto the saddle of his horse.

"Araxys!" he yelled.

His father's killer looked at him and snarled. Then he drew his sword and dug his heels into the horses' sides, spurring it into a gallop towards him.

He was unarmed and defenceless.

Araxys must have noticed, and he flashed him a wicked smile as his horse bore down.

He waited until the last second then rolled to his side, narrowly avoiding the sweep of the blade as the Elf brought it down. Picking himself up from the dust, he watched as his nemesis drove his steed up the slope and along the line of the ridge to escape.

Dirk glanced toward the carriage.

There were two horses left.

If he could untether one, he could use it to pursue him.

He dashed over, throwing a cursory glance toward Bakker and his men, who were engaged in a fierce melee with the remaining Rebels.

On the other side of the carriage, he saw Marfine climbing up onto her horse to escape. Varek was sneaking up behind her with his sword.

Without a second thought, Dirk veered towards him, throwing himself at the Guildsman's legs, tackling him to the ground. As he fell, the weapon flew from his hands, burying itself point first in the dirt.

Varek hissed and looked back at him.

Dirk responded by punching him in the face.

"Go!" he shouted to Marfine.

The She-Elf looked down at him from the saddle.

It wasn't clear if she wanted to thank him or kill him, but either way she flicked the reins of her horse and raced off in the direction of her father, who was now disappearing beyond the ridge.

"Stupid boy," Varek growled, wiping the blood from his mouth. "You'll pay for this!"

He launched a fist at Dirk's face.

The blow caught him cleanly on the chin and the force knocked him backwards.

Varek then pounced upon him, pinning him down and battering him with a flurry of punches. One of the strikes caught Dirk's in the ear, causing it to ring like a bell inside of his head.

Another punch came down.

This one caught him on the temple.

For a second or two, Dirk lost consciousness, and his arms dropped to his sides.

He recovered just in time to see the northerner above him, sporting a twisted smile of victory.

"Time to die," he sneered, raising up his arms to finish him.

Dirk had no time to think.

Acting on pure instinct, he reached up and seized the shaft of the arrow that was protruding from Varek's shoulder. The Guildsman shrieked and flinched. The movement dislodged the bolt and Dirk thrust its point through the bottom of the man's chin.

Varek spluttered then clawed at the shaft with his hands. His fingers found the flight and he pulled it out, spattering Dirk with a fountain of blood. He then gargled horribly and fell onto his side, dead.

Dirk got to his feet and looked behind him.

Bakker, Kort and Mu'Ungo had defeated the other rebels. They were looking over and had noticed the body of Varek beside him. Bakker roared and raised his blade.

Dirk was on his feet in an instant.

He ran over to the front of the carriage, grabbed the reins of the stallion at the front and climbed up onto its back.

As Bakker and the others neared, he kicked his heels into the horse's side. The horse turned in the dirt, knocking the three men off their feet. He then spurred his mount forward, snatching up Varek's blade as he raced up the ridge in pursuit of Araxys.

CHAPTER 13

The stallion was strong and rode at a fierce pace. It was much faster than the steeds favoured by the Elves, which had been raised in the heat and were built for endurance.

Following the line of the ridge, he soon caught sight of Araxys up ahead.

Tapping the Stallion's rump with the flat of his sword, Dirk's steed found an extra burst of pace, and it snorted wildly as it thundered forward, closing the gap between them.

Araxys glanced back and saw him. He snarled then yelled at his mare to go faster.

The path narrowed as it wound its way around the edge of a butte. Conscious of the sheer drop, Dirk guided his stallion to the right... Then crashed into the mare that had drawn up alongside him!

His stallion lost its footing momentarily, stumbling on the broken path. Dirk shifted his weight in the saddle and glanced to his right.

It was Marfine.

She'd appeared from nowhere and was attempting to slow him down by bringing her steed alongside his.

"What are you doing?" he shouted.

The look on her face told him everything he needed to know.

She looked furious, betrayed.

She drew a dagger from her belt and in a single swift motion, buried the blade into the rump of Dirk's ride. The Stallion roared in pain, then bucked him from the seat.

He fell through the air and crashed down onto the edge of

the ridge, nearly falling over the side. The horse grunted angrily then turned and ran away. As Dirk got to his feet, Marfine reined in her mount.

"Father!" she yelled at the escaping Araxys.

The Elf glanced over his shoulder and smiled. He slowed his mount to a trot then swung it round and began riding back, building up speed as he came.

He passed by his daughter, flashing her an angry look.

He was disappointed with her.

It was obvious why.

She'd deceived him; defied his orders by not killing Dirk as she'd promised. Whether she was his daughter or not, it was a crime that would not go unpunished.

He then switched his focus to Dirk and lashed the reins of his mount, spurring his steed into a charge.

This time he couldn't roll away. He was trapped on the edge with nowhere to go. Nothing, it seemed, could stop him from being run down.

There was no escape.

Or was there…?

As the Elf raised his sword to cut him in two, Dirk stepped off the edge and allowed himself to drop, twisting as he fell.

Araxys' blade swished past his head as he reached out his hands and seized hold of the ledge to stop him falling. The sudden stop swung his torso into the wall of the cliff, and he glanced down to see his legs dangling above the sheer drop.

Araxys' horse whinnied, and the Elf grunted in frustration. Dirk watched from the precipice as he climbed down from his saddle and strode over to where he was hanging.

"Slippery scum," he yelled, his one good eye filled with fury. "I'll murder you like I murdered your thieving sire."

He approached the edge and lifted his blade.

Dirk closed his eyes.

I'm sorry father, he whispered to himself.

I failed you.

Suddenly, he heard the Elf shriek.

Dirk opened his eyes and saw Araxys stumbling backwards, reaching for his back. He then fell to the ground and turned over, and Dirk noticed the hilt of a dagger sticking out of his back. He glanced up and saw Marfine staring down at her father from her saddle.

"Why?" Araxys gasped.

"You lied to me," she said. "You promised we were on the side of right."

Araxys' face contorted into a grimace, a mixture of pain and frustration.

"Naïve fool," he sneered. "War makes monsters of us all."

She clicked her tongue dismissively.

Araxys closed his eyes then slumped lifelessly to the floor.

The killer of his father was dead.

Justice had been served.

But why didn't it feel like it?

His desire for revenge had been sated, yet he still felt empty, unsatisfied.

He hauled himself up and looked at the She-Elf sitting in the saddle of her horse.

She glared at him then blew out her cheeks.

Without saying a word, she flicked the reins of her mare and rode it away down the line of the ridge.

Dirk wondered what was going through her mind...

Her ideals had been shattered. She'd believed the Elves were fighting a just cause and were fighting it well. But her father's admission that he'd murdered a man in cold blood challenged that. She'd been lied to, deceived, by a man she thought she could trust...

As she disappeared in a cloud of dust, he realised that his own father had deceived him in a similar way. The coin in the cart that they were taking to Hellenburg belonged to Araxys, and he had killed him for stealing it.

At once, he felt empty and unfulfilled.

This wasn't justice.

He suddenly realised what the passage in the She-En

meant.

Marfine had been right when she'd said the meaning would come to him in time.

It had.

"I see you've gotten what you wanted..."

Bakker's voice alarmed Dirk.

In the chaos of the chase, he'd forgotten the Vipers were on his tail.

He turned and saw the three of them behind him, sitting smugly in the saddles of their horses. Mu'Ungo and Kort were staring at him, but Bakker's eyes were fixed upon on the body of the fallen Rebel Leader.

"...But we're the ones who'll be claiming his head..."

He turned his focus to Dirk.

"...Yours too."

They dismounted and drew their swords.

Kort smiled wickedly as he circled the air with his Hunter's Bite.

"No Elves to save you this time," he sneered.

The three of them came forward.

Dirk backed away, holding up his hands.

He quickly scanned the ground for his sword, which he'd dropped after his horse had bucked. It was lying a good twenty feet from where he was standing.

There was no way he could get to it.

He stepped back and raised his hands, then at once all three of them rushed forward. Outnumbered and unarmed, there was nothing more he could do but drop to his knees and face his demise.

"Pick him up," Bakker ordered. "I want him to look me in the eye when I kill him."

Mu'Ungo lifted him up and then pinned his arms behind his back.

Bakker stepped forward, sheathed his sword, and drew the dagger from his belt.

"Hold him steady while I cut his throat," he said, as he

raised his knife.

"Yes, Dark One," Kort added. "Don't let him go this time."

The big man growled.

Dirk got the feeling he'd had enough of being insulted.

Kort's words had been the final straw.

Mu'Ungo threw him aside and launched himself at the Grexian, shoulder-charging him to the floor. With a mighty roar, he climbed upon the man and began pummelling him with his fists.

The wily Westrener responded by raking the serrated edge of his blade against the Southerner's back. Mu'Ungo howled then stepped back.

"Stop it both of you!" Bakker yelled.

But the duel was far from done.

The Kulaanian lunged forward but Kort quickly rolled out of the way as he brought down his blade.

Dirk glanced to his left and saw his *Hunter's Bite.*

Bakker saw him looking.

In a flash, he began scrambling towards it.

The Guildsergeant went for it too.

As Bakker bore down on him, Dirk dropped his shoulder and forward rolled toward his blade, snatching it up as he planted his feet upon the bone-dry earth.

He stood up and raised his weapon.

Bakker sneered.

He sheathed his dagger and drew his sword.

"What a waste," he said, coming forward. "You had so much potential."

Bakker suddenly lunged forward, flicking the point of his blade towards Dirk's face. Dirk stepped aside, dodging the strike, then responded with a thrust of his own, which the Guildsergeant swatted away with ease.

The man stepped back, shaking his head.

"You would have made such a fine addition to our unit," he lamented. "You're brave, ballsy, full of spunk… It's a shame you chose your vows over glory."

He darted forward, this time sweeping his blade horizontally towards Dirk's side. Dirk raised his sword and parried.

"Stupid boy," he spat, as the steel of their blades ground together. "I could have turned you into a real Guildsman."

"Guildsmen keep their vows," Dirk replied, pushing him away.

Bakker stepped back and laughed.

"Did you not learn anything?" he sneered. "The vows we took are meaningless."

"To you maybe," Dirk replied. "Not me."

He rushed forward and swung his blade at Bakker's side. The Guildsergeant anticipated the move and dodged to his right. Before Dirk could react, the man thrust his blade forward.

The point speared Dirk's shoulder.

He paced backwards and glanced down at the wound. Blood streamed from it, staining the grey of his tunic a dark shade of red.

Bakker grinned victoriously.

It was understandable.

He was stronger, faster and by far the better swordsman.

The Guildsergeant came forward and Dirk backed away.

He was unsure of himself, scared.

He could feel his heart beating in his chest.

He took another step backwards.

Bakker lifted his sword and charged.

Dirk reacted by side-stepping to his left but the Guildsergeant checked his stride and turned, then swept his blade upwards in a wide arc.

Dirk stumbled backwards.

He felt pain above his right knee.

He looked down and saw that he was bleeding from his thigh.

Bakker smiled and began wheeling around him.

He looked confident, as if the fight was all but over.

"By the time I'm through with you," he said. "You're going to wish I'd have cut your throat."

His bravado was palpable.

He was certain of victory.

Bakker looked him in the eye and grinned wickedly.

He came forward once more.

Dirk stepped back… and tripped over the body of Araxys.

As he crashed to the ground, his sword fell from his hand, and clattered across the path and then disappeared over the edge of the cliff.

Lying on his back and with nothing to defend himself, Dirk watched in horror as Bakker came forward to finish him off.

Just then, Dirk noticed something shiny near his feet.

It was Araxys' sabre, it's hilt propped up against the Rebel Leader's thigh. As Bakker bore down on him, he lifted his boot and brought his heel down upon it. The blade of the Elf's sword sprang upwards and the Guildsergeant's momentum carried him into it. The man yelped in pain as the Elven steel bit deeply into his thigh, stopping him in his tracks.

Seizing the initiative, Dirk leant forward and swung a punch at Bakker's face. His fist connected with the man's chin, and he stumbled backwards and dropped to his knees. Dirk picked himself up and aimed a kick at the Guildsergeant's sword-hand, sending his blade flying across the earth. Bakker snarled then reached for the dagger at his belt, but Dirk quickly seized his wrist and twisted it inwards. Bakker hissed and released the blade, and Dirk snatched it up and held it to his throat.

"Go on," Bakker snarled. "Finish it."

Dirk shook his head and dragged the man to his feet.

"No," he replied. "I'm not like you."

Bakker chuckled.

"Too bad," he laughed, gesturing behind them. "He is…"

Dirk turned and saw Mu'Ungo rising to his feet over Kort's lifeless body.

"I suggest you let me go," Bakker sneered, as the big man started walking over. "This won't end well otherwise… I've seen him crush a man's skull with his bare hands."

The Kulaanian came within two paces of them then stopped.

"Well?" his master yelled. "What are you waiting for? Help me!"

Dirk noticed the big man's eyes.

They were welling with tears.

"No," Mu'Ungo said.

He stepped forward and seized the Guildsergeant's hands.

"What are you doing, man?" the officer growled. "I gave you an order!"

"I'm not your slave anymore," Mu'Ungo replied.

He took the manacles from his belt and snapped them in place around Bakker's wrists.

Dirk turned him round.

"You're under arrest," he said.

Bakker sniffed.

"On what charge?"

"Murder," Dirk replied.

The Guildsergeant smirked.

"Good luck making it stick," he said. "It's your word against mine..."

"We'll see about that," Dirk replied, gesturing to the ridge-line.

Bakker turned and saw the troop of riders rumbling toward them. All wore the grey jackets of the Guild, but their shoulders of their tunics were topped with silver epaulettes.

It was the Guild Corps.

As they neared, Dirk saw Coen among them.

"Where have you been?" Dirk shouted. "You were supposed to be here an hour ago."

"You weren't where you said you'd be," Coen replied as he dismounted his horse. "But lucky for you we picked up your tracks..."

Dirk handed Bakker to Mu'Ungo.

"Better late than never," he remarked.

Coen laughed then came to him with open arms.

"I wasn't expecting to see you so soon," he said.

"Me neither," Dirk replied, as he hugged him warmly. "It's good to see you, friend."

Coen's comrades got down from their horses and made their way over to Bakker and the big man.

"Not him," Dirk said, pointing to the Kulaanian. "He's a witness."

The Corpsmen nodded and seized just Bakker.

"I take it you got my letter?" Dirk said to Coen.

"I did," he replied. "Sounds like a nasty business you've got yourself caught up in.... I told you Ghis was dangerous."

"You wouldn't know the half of it," Dirk replied.

He turned and looked at Bakker, who sneered at him as the Corpsmen marched him away.

"This isn't over," the Guildsergeant warned, smiling wickedly as he was lifted up onto one of the horses. "Far from it..."

"What'll happen to him?" Dirk asked Coen.

"He'll stand trial at the Guildcourt in Einhof," he replied.

"Good," Dirk said.

"You'll need to be there too..." Coen added. "...As a witness."

CHAPTER 14

The courtroom at Einhof was cold and Dirk shivered as he took to the witness stand.

Bakker stood in the Defendant's box across the room, flanked by two ushers of the court. His hands and feet were chained, and he was wearing the black and white stripes of a prisoner.

Stripped of his title and uniform, he looked a shadow of his former self. Prior to his internment he'd cut a fine figure amongst his peers. Now he appeared thin, gaunt and pitiful.

The Magistrate, a stern middle-aged man with huge jowls that hung below his chin, called for the Clerk to conduct the swear-in, and the man brought a copy of the Testament to Dirk's lectern.

"I'll use this instead," he said before the man spoke. He reached inside his tunic and pulled out his copy the She-En.

The Justice nodded and Dirk placed his hand on the book's ravaged cover.

"Do you swear to tell nothing but the truth in the eyes of your God?" the man said.

"I do," Dirk confirmed.

The Clerk nodded then returned to his seat. The Magistrate then asked Dirk to provide his testimony.

Dirk then gave his account of what had happened, describing in detail the events leading up and including the massacre at Shafarr.

There were gasps from the audience as he told the Court how Bakker had slit the throat of one of the villagers, and some of the Guildsmen watching from the gallery had to be ejected by ushers after hurling obscenities at the defendant for breaking his vows.

Once Dirk had finished, the Magistrate dismissed him from the stand and he went to watch the rest of the proceedings from the stalls.

After a brief recess, Mu'Ungo was called to the witness box and asked to give his version of events.

The Kulaanian began by describing how he'd originally met Bakker in Tibrut, after the Guildsergeant had brought his freedom from a crew of Reavers, who'd enslaved him since he was a boy.

"He gave me my freedom," the big man testified, "So in return I did as he said."

He went on to describe how Bakker had enlisted him at the Guildschool in Marmur and offered him employment in Ghis after *Passing Out.*

"He told me to forget everything the Guild had taught me..." the big man said. "...That the vows I took were useless in the real world and that my only loyalty should be to him."

He then outlined how Bakker had created the Red Vipers, a handpicked group of thugs who, for one reason or another, had never been able to settle into any Guild.

"Are you saying he chose them for their rambunctiousness?" asked the Prosecutor, a handsome young lawyer named Vor Ruis.

"No," Mu'Ungo replied. "For their savagery."

When asked to explain further, the Kulaanian described how the other members of the group – Varek, Ermus, Kort, and Boors – had all previously been investigated by the Guild Corps for charges relating to the improper treatment of prisoners.

"Why did Bakker feel they were the right men for him?" the counsel asked.

"Because he liked his enemies to suffer," Mu'Ungo replied. "He wanted men who could make that happen."

"And what did he offer in return?"

"A family," Mu'Ungo replied.

The Defence Counsel, who all this time had been standing next to Bakker in the defendant's box, suddenly stood up and raised his hand.

"A question, M'Lord, if I may?" he said to the Magistrate.

The Justice nodded and prompted him to speak.

He stepped forward and looked Mu'Ungo in the eye.

"So why, in the end, after all this man had done for you," he began, "did you suddenly decide to turn against him?"

It was a shrewd question.

Mu'Ungo had had a good life under Bakker.

Of that there was no doubt.

The Guildsergeant had bought his freedom, procured him employment, put a roof over his head, and cut him into a share of the Viper's booty...

Many would think him to fool to give it up.

But Mu'Ungo had an answer.

"Because I was still a slave in all but name," he said.

The court fell silent.

Dirk glanced over to Bakker, who was shaking his head in the dock.

"I see," the Defence Counsel offered. "So at what *precise* point did you realise this?"

Mu'Ungo gave him a cursory look, as if he didn't understand the question.

"Let me clarify," the Counsel added, "Was it before or after the arrival of the Guild Corps?"

"Before," the Kulaanian replied.

"How *long* before?" the Defender asked. "Months, Weeks, Days... Less?"

Mu'Ungo shifted on his feet.

"Less," he replied.

"How many hours?" he asked. "Or was it a matter of minutes?"

Mu'Ungo said nothing.

His silence was enough to condemn him.

The Counsel smirked.

"No further questions," he said.

The Magistrate dismissed Mu'Ungo from the stand and called for the court to recess.

Dirk left the room and found Coen waiting outside. The Corpsman had been watching the proceedings from the gallery. He looked tense.

"What's wrong?" Dirk asked.

"I don't think there's enough evidence to convict," Coen sighed.

"How so?" Dirk asked.

"As it stands, it's your word against his."

"But there are two of us."

"The southerner's testimony is flawed," Coen responded.

"Why?" Dirk asked. "He was there. He saw what happened."

"He may have," his friend replied. "But he could also be saying this to extricate himself from blame."

Dirk glared at him.

"He's not lying," he spat.

"You and I know that" Coen replied. "But will the Magistrate?"

Dirk snorted.

"So he's going to get away with it?"

Coen sighed.

"It'll all come down to which one of you the Magistrate believes," he said. "I know it's hard for you to hear but we have no evidence."

"No evidence?" Dirk rasped. "What about Shafarr? Did you not go there and see what happened?"

"We did," Coen replied. "But there was nothing to see."

"What do you mean?" Dirk asked.

"The village, and everything in it, had been razed to the ground," Coen said.

Dirk sighed.

They'd gone back and finished the job.

"Where there any survivors?" he replied.

Coen shook his head.

"We managed to track a few down in Shemali," he said. "But they all refused to speak."

"Why?" Dirk asked.

"They said they didn't trust us."

It was understandable.

They were scared.

And after what Bakker and his men had done, it wasn't surprising.

"What about Ghis?" Dirk asked. "Surely you must have found someone there. The Vipers had a network of informants. One of them must have talked."

"They'd all left the city," Coen replied. "Even your man, Ruyven."

Dirk's eyes drifted to the floor.

He couldn't believe what he was hearing.

There was a chance Bakker would go unpunished.

"Listen, don't be too disheartened," Coen said. "It may all go our way. Justice Arneld is a good man. He knows how to sniff out a lie when he hears one."

"I know a lie when I hear one too," Dirk said, sadly.

Coen responded with a weak smile.

It was clear what he thought of their chances...

A bell rang in the hall.

It was a call for everyone to return to the courtroom, as the session was about to restart.

Expelling a long sigh, Dirk turned and made his way back inside the chamber.

* * *

Once everyone was back inside, the Defence Counsel approached the Judge's bench and formally requested for Bakker to take the stand.

Justice Arneld held down his wig while he nodded, then signalled to the ushers to bring the man to the witness box.

Bakker shuffled pitifully as he was taken from the dock.

Dirk suspected he'd deliberately starved himself during his internment so as to appear weaker and more harmless.

It was nothing more than optics, but the tactic seemed to have worked for he heard sympathetic muttering from some of the citizens sitting beside him.

Once Bakker had stepped up into the lectern, the Clerk came forward with a copy of the Testament.

"Do you swear to tell nothing but the truth in the eyes of your God?" he asked.

"I do," Bakker replied. "And may Tekat take my soul if not."

The Clerk nodded then returned to his seat. The Defence Counsel stood up and asked Bakker to state his version of events.

It came as no surprise that everything he said was a lie.

He spoke precisely and concisely.

It was clear he'd been coached.

"When we got to the village," he began, "we found that it had already been desecrated. We looked around for survivors. Guildsman Vanslow and Mu'Ungo were paired together and they found a woman in one of the houses. They brought her outside and began interrogating her. When she refused to cooperate, they tied her to the obelisk and began torturing her. When she still refused to talk, they slit her throat."

A collective gasp went up from the Gallery.

The Prosecution counsel immediately raised his hand and the Magistrate gestured for him to speak.

"As I understand it," he began, "You were in command, were you not?"

"I was," Bakker replied.

"So why, if this *alleged* crime was happening under your nose, did you do nothing to stop it?"

"I tried," Bakker stated. "As soon as I saw what was happening, I ordered him to stand down. But Guildsman Vanslow refused to listen."

He turned his head and looked directly at Dirk.

"That's when he ran the blade across her throat."

Lies, Dirk thought.

Pure lies.

The audience began to murmur, and the Magistrate called for order. Once things had quieted down, he gestured for the Counsel to continue.

"You make some bold claims," the Prosecutor began. "But are we to believe that Guildsman Vanslow did what he did out of pure bloodlust? That he was so *incensed* by the suspect's refusal to speak, that he tortured, then killed her?"

Bakker started to speak but Vor raised his hand.

"Before you answer..." he added, "...may I remind you that this is the *same person* who, despite having reason to kill you when you attacked him, chose to arrest you instead..."

"I never said he was driven by that," Bakker replied.

"Then what was driven by?" the Prosecutor asked.

"Revenge," Bakker said.

The Prosecutor raised an eyebrow.

"Revenge?" he said, somewhat unimpressed. "And what, pray tell, did this old dear do to him that warranted such a violent reaction?"

"He believed she knew the whereabouts of his father's killer."

A roar went up from the Gallery.

Bakker continued over the din.

"...He was obsessed with finding him. He was a boy when it happened. It had haunted him all his life..."

The Magistrate struck the gavel with his hammer.

"Order!" he shouted in response to the rumpus. "Order!"

When the noise failed to abate, he called a recess.

Dirk stormed out of chamber and kicked the wall of the corridor with his boot.

"Easy," Coen said, placing a hand on his shoulder.

"Why is he allowed to do that?" Dirk rasped. "He's lying about me to the whole court!"

"He's entitled to have his say," the blonde-haired Guildsman replied.

"Really?" Dirk replied. "After what he did to those people?"

He held his head in his hands, reliving the scene.

"...If only you could have seen it. He rounded them up and butchered them one by one..."

"I'm sure the Magistrate will see through it," Coen argued. "His testimony bordered on the ridiculous. To suggest you were motivated by revenge seems totally absurd...."

Dirk gave him a knowing look.

Coen's jaw dropped.

"No..." he exclaimed. "It's true?"

Dirk nodded.

"My father was killed by an Elf," he admitted. "But that doesn't mean I killed that woman."

Coen raised his hand to his mouth.

He suddenly looked worried.

"What?" Dirk asked.

"It gives you motive," Coen replied.

He looked Dirk in the eye.

"Who else knows this?"

Dirk shook his head.

"I'm not sure," he said.

"Well let's just pray no one comes out of the woodwork," Coen replied. "Your life depends on it."

"What do you mean?" Dirk replied. "I'm not the one on trial."

"This is a *Guild* Court..." Coen replied.

Dirk looked at him blankly.

"Everyone in that chamber is on Trial."

* * *

Dirk stared into Bakker's eyes as he waited for the Magistrate to return. The Guildsergeant looked so weak and vulnerable, and he wondered how easy it would be to vault the stalls, storm over to the dock and plunge his dagger into his evil heart...

No, a voice in his head told him.

It wouldn't be justice.

It wouldn't calm his heart.

Dirk bit his lip and waited.

The Defence counsel glanced at the Prosecution Lawyer as he approached the bench. There was a cunning look in his eyes and Dirk wondered what he was up to.

"The Defence would like to call a witness," he declared.

"So be it," the Magistrate replied.

The Counsel turned and signalled to the ushers who were standing at the door. They nodded back then opened the panels to reveal the grizzled form of Major Patz.

Dirk's heart skipped a beat, as he suddenly remembered his conversation with the man prior to his transfer to Ghis, and how he'd granted his request after speaking of his father's killer.

He glanced across the hall to Coen and shook his head.

The young Corpsman responded by crossing his palms over his mouth.

Things didn't look good.

After taking the stand and swearing on the Testament, the Defence Counsel approached Patz at the witness box.

"Please state your name for the Clerk," he said.

"Major Mieter Patz," the man replied.

"And what is the nature of the relationship to the key witness?"

"I mentored him for six years at the Guild School of Royal Kronnig."

"And would you describe yourself as 'close' to Guildsman Vanslow?"

"No," Patz replied.

"And how would you describe him as a student?"

"Unremarkable," the Major replied.

"So, there's no prior history between you, no reason or motive, for you to denigrate his character in any way?"

The question was somewhat wordy but served its purpose.

"No," Patz replied. "Like I said, he was unremarkable."

"So, given your lack of familiarity with Guildsman Vanslow," he continued, "why do you think you've been called here today?"

"I believe it has something to do with our conversation prior to his transfer."

"Please elaborate," the Counsel replied.

Patz described how Dirk had visited him in his chambers and had asked him to be stationed in Ghis.

"Ghis?" the Defence counsel exclaimed. "A strange choice for a new recruit, wouldn't you agree?"

"Yes," Patz said.

"Just to give the Court some context," the Counsel added, "how many recruits, on average, would you say choose to spend their first year of service there?"

"None," Patz replied.

The Defence counsel feigned shock.

"I see," he said. "So, when Guildsman Vanslow came to you with this request, did he tell you why he wanted to go to a place *so dangerous*, that not a single recruit had been assigned there before?"

The Prosecutor stood and raised his hand.

"I object to this line of questioning," he retorted. "Major Patz has already admitted he did not know the recruit well. If that's the case, how could he possibly know what was going on inside his mind?"

The Magistrate shook his head.

"That wasn't the question," he said. "The Defence asked whether Vanslow *stated* his reason."

The Prosecutor returned to his seat, casting an awkward glance in Dirk's direction.

The Counsel smiled then took a pace forward.

"Well, Major Patz?" he asked. "Did he?"

"He did," the man replied.

"And what did he say?"

The Major's eyes found Dirk in the gallery.

"He said he wanted to find the man who'd killed his father."

Dirk heard gasps, tuts and curses from the people sitting all around him.

The Defence counsel smiled.

"No further questions," he said.

Dirk bit down on his tongue.

He hadn't been this furious since that fateful day in the Silent Valley...

It seemed Bakker hadn't been lying when he'd said it wasn't over.

Now he knew why.

He was being set up.

No wonder the bastard looked so smug.

His plan had played out perfectly.

Dirk chewed on his lip as the Prosecutor stood up to cross-examine the witness.

"Major," he began, "we all heard how, despite six years of mentoring, you didn't consider yourself close to recruit Vanslow... But can you now describe to this court your relationship with the Defendant?"

Patz didn't flinch.

The question was crucial.

It established they were friends.

The Major leaned forward.

"We served together," he answered.

"Yes," the Prosecution Counsel finished, glancing at his notes. "In the Drum Brigade."

Dirk had heard of the Drum. They were regiment in the Hessellian Army comprised of entirely foreign troops. Service was for life but if you joined, you were absolved of any crimes you may have committed in the past. The only way of leaving was through honourable discharge, usually granted for acts of exceptional bravery.

"...And then thereafter for the Guild in Ghis?" Vor continued.

"Yes," Patz replied.

"So, would you describe your relationship as 'close'?"

"No," Patz replied.

"Yet you served together, fought together, lived together?"

"I was his Officer, and he was my charge," Patz replied.

He was lying.

Dirk could see it in his eyes.

"Is it not true he once saved your life?" Vor asked.

"Yes," the Major replied.

"And would you say such an event would bring two people closer, or make them more distant?"

"Closer," Patz admitted.

"So how close were you?" the Prosecutor asked. "Close enough to lie for him?"

The Defence Counsel raised his hand.

"I object to this line of questioning," the man said. "The witness has already given an answer to the question of his relationship with the defendant."

The Magistrate looked thoughtful.

"Sustained," he said finally. "This man is a hero of Hessell and Gerwald. You will treat him with the respect he deserves."

"But M'Lord," Vor pleaded. "The question is pertinent to the case. It provides a motive for collaboration."

"I'm well aware of what you're trying to suggest, Counsel," the Magistrate replied. "But the witness has already answered."

The Prosecutor expelled a frustrated sigh.

"So, Major," he continued, taking a different tack, "Given that you knew the defendant in a *professional* capacity, how would you describe him as a Guildsman?"

"A good one," Patz replied.

"Why?"

"He always did what was expected of him."

"And was that always within the confines of your vows?"

Dirk noticed Patz glance at Bakker.

"Always," he replied.

"By your recollection..." Vor Ruis continued. "...Was there any occasion when the Guildsergeant expressed a desire to overstep his remit?"

"Never," Patz answered. "Like I said, he was a good Guildsman. He was honest and true, respectful of his vows."

"Yet we've heard testimonies here that suggest the opposite... Are you saying those witnesses are lying?"

"If that's what you want me to say," Patz replied.

"And why would they lie?"

"I think that's something you should ask them."

He glanced up at the Magistrate, who then glared at the Prosecutor.

"Counsel," he began, "Unless you have something more substantial to ask, I suggest you dismiss the witness."

Ruis shook his head.

"No further questions," he said through gritted teeth.

Dirk watched as Patz left the stand and made his way out of the court.

His testimony had made a difference.

Of that there was no doubt.

He'd painted a picture of Bakker as a decent man, devoid of ill intent. He'd also confirmed Dirk's motives for seeking employ in Ghis.

It would be hard for a reasonable man not to conclude from this that it should be Dirk, not Bakker, sitting in the dock.

With both sides' witnesses now heard, the Magistrate called the session to a close and instructed the Court that his verdict would be given in the morning.

Before he dismissed the Court, he called upon the ushers to detain the witnesses in the cells as a precaution against their non-appearance.

As he finished speaking, Dirk noticed Bakker staring at him from the dock.

His mouth was parted, his lips upturned into a wicked smile.

It was a look of victory...

A look that said he'd won...

CHAPTER 15

Coen came to visit him later that night in the holding cell beneath the Courthouse. The man's sorrowful expression reflected Dirk's own feelings.

No words needed to be said when he arrived.

It was clear how he felt.

"I'm sorry, Dirk," he said, after sitting down beside him on his bunk. "But I can't see a way out of this."

Dirk sighed.

He knew his friend was right.

"What am I looking at?" Dirk asked.

The question of his guilt was moot.

Coen shook his head.

"At best you're looking at expulsion from the Guild," he replied.

"And at worst?"

"A long stretch in *Grente Clink*."

In accordance with the *Finder's Covenant*, all convicted Guildsmen served their sentences in Hessell. Grente Clink was somewhat of a misnomer. The 'prison' was actually a sandstone mine near the Hussfaltian border, and there were no locked cells.

"How long?" Dirk asked.

"The standard term is twenty-five years," Coen replied.

Dirk knew he'd last no more than ten.

The mine was notorious for its violence. Beatings by guards and other inmates were rife, and it was said that a lengthy stay 'within the pit' was akin to a death sentence.

"Is there anything you can do for me?" Dirk asked.

Coen shook his head.

"I can plead for clemency," he said, "But it won't amount to much coming from someone like myself."

"What about your father?" Dirk suggested.

"He wouldn't get involved," the man replied. "Besides, what would he say? He doesn't know you."

"But you do," Dirk said. "You could speak to him, put in a word for me…"

"It wouldn't wash with the court," Coen replied.

Dirk held his head in his hands.

"How did it ever come to this?" he lamented. "I did the right thing. Now I'm being punished for it."

Coen sighed.

"You need a witness," the man said. "Someone who can attest you weren't driven by revenge."

Dirk shook his head.

"I can't believe no one came forward from the village," he muttered.

"It's a sign of the times," Coen replied. "Everyone's too afraid. They'd rather live in a safe world than a just one. Personally, I blame the Priests. For too long they've sat back while apathy reigns. It's one of the reasons I joined the Corps."

"To stem the tide?"

Coen nodded.

"Even if it's a losing cause?" Dirk asked.

Coen smiled sadly.

"Sometimes it's the fight that's important."

He stayed with Dirk for a further hour or so before the Gaoler came to the door and asked him to leave.

"You'll visit me in Hessell?" Dirk asked, as Coen made his way out.

"Of course," his friend replied. "And I'll carry on fighting to get you justice."

"Thank you," Dirk replied.

Coen smiled then left, and the gaoler locked the door behind him.

Dirk sat back on his bunk and took out his copy of the She'En, looking for the prayer the Elves said to implore the Goddess for help. When he found it, he was surprised to find it also contained instructions on what to do.

He climbed down from his bunk and knelt on the floor. Then he extended his arms to the heavens and read aloud the passage from the page and bent his torso forward into a bow, touching the floor of his cell with his fingertips.

He'd never prayed this like before.

Then again why not?

All his life he'd been praying to V'Loire.

Not once had he answered.

Maybe Sheenah would...?

CHAPTER 16

Dirk glanced at Bakker, who was standing beside him in the dock. He was staring ahead, wearing an innocent look on his face. Dirk turned his head to the gallery, which was overflowing with people.

It came as no surprise.

Word of the trial and the drama that was unfolding had piqued much interest, and the story had travelled far and wide.

Before he'd been brought out of his cell, the Gaoler had asked him to sign a copy of the local newssheet; a rag entitled the *Einhof Gazette.* The man had been especially nice to him and wished him luck on the verdict.

"You're quite the celebrity now," the man had told him. "We're all rooting for you."

Dirk hadn't believed a word of it.

He'd seen the faces of the public as he'd been led out the previous day.

Many believed he was guilty.

He scanned the rows of seats looking for Coen, and eventually found his face among the stalls. His arms were crossed, and he seemed anxious.

Once the gallery had been filled, the Clerk of the court rose to his feet and asked everyone to stand for the Magistrate, who then emerged from the door to his chambers.

The Justice bore a solemn look on his long face as he walked over to his throne. Once there, he bade everyone to sit then raised his hand to address the room.

"Before I reveal my verdict," he said, "Are there any further witnesses to be called by either counsel?"

The Defence Counsel rose to his feet.

"No further witnesses from the Defence," he said.

"And the Prosecution?"

Vor Ruis stood up slowly.

"No, M'Lord," he said.

The words tumbled from his lips.

He looked beaten, defeated.

He'd given it his best shot but had fallen at the last hurdle, defeated by the Guild's failure to produce any evidence.

"Very well," the Magistrate replied. "In that case, I will begin my verdict."

From his teachings in Guildschool, Dirk knew that Guild Law, unlike the 'common' law practiced throughout Gerwald and Westren, required Magistrates to deliver narrative verdicts, which fully explained their decision-making. The custom ensured transparency of the Justice's thought-process and served to explain how and why they had reached their conclusion.

They were also very long and convoluted.

"The matter brought before me," the Justice began, "was to decide the innocence or guilt of Ermus Bakker, serving Sergeant of the Ghisian Guild, in respect of the alleged murder of the citizens of the village of Shafarr in Gefghed."

He took a breath.

"However, during the course of this trial, counter-allegations were made by the Defence, which questioned the innocence of the original plaintiffs, and as a result, we now find ourselves in a position where there are three defendants rather than one."

The Magistrate's protracted opening drew chuckles from certain sections of the gallery. They were probably used to hearing the shorter verdicts delivered by regular Judges and found it all quite humorous.

After listening to Arneld's turgid diatribe, Dirk was inclined to agree.

"This case has been a difficult one," the Magistrate continued. "Due to lack of evidence presented by both sides, my decision-making was limited to the testimonies of witnesses from both the Prosecution and the Defence. And it is upon these statements alone that I draw my conclusion."

Get on with it, Dirk thought.

The verdict was clear.

There was no point dragging it out for the sake of pomp.

"And so," the Justice said, finally turning his head to look at them, "I shall now deliver my verdict."

Finally...

"Ermus Bakker," the Magistrate began. "You adequately explained your actions and provided a counterargument to the plaintiff's case, which was strengthened but the additional testimony of your witness."

No surprises, Dirk thought.

"However," the Justice continued. "I found your personal testimony unconvincing. I strongly suspect that you lied to this court on many occasions, but in the absence of any hard evidence to support my belief, I'm bound by my duty as a servant of the Law to find you not guilty in the eyes of this Court."

The decision was met with stifled murmurs.

It was a sure sign most people agreed with the Justice's decision.

Dirk glanced to his right and saw the Guildsergeant smirking.

He'd got exactly what he'd wanted.

The Magistrate then turned his attention to Dirk and Mu'Ungo, who was also present in the dock.

Dirk glanced at the Kulaanian to his left. The big man looked unworried at the prospect of losing his freedom.

It was understandable given the fact he'd spent most of his life either enslaved or under the thrall of Bakker.

"Guildsman Mu'Ungo," he began. "I found your testimony to be frank and honest, but in absence of hard evidence to support your claims, I could not rely on it to make a judgement as the nature of the Defendant's Guilt."

The big man stared ahead blankly, and his stoic reaction

made Dirk wonder whether he'd anticipated this outcome from the start.

"However," the Justice continued, "During the course of this trial, you freely admitted to a number of infractions you committed whilst wearing the Iron Seal. In respect of these crimes, hard evidence would normally be required to substantiate them, however since this information was deigned to the Court by admission, I have no choice but to accept your testimony as a confession."

Dirk shook his head and looked to the Prosecution Counsel; whose eyes were fixed on the floor.

There was nothing untoward here…

"…As such," he concluded, "I hereby find you guilty of breaking the Vow of Honour, and for this I sentence you to no less than twenty-five years imprisonment."

The citizens in the gallery gasped.

Dirk was not surprised.

He'd thought it would have been obvious to the Magistrate that there was not a shred of malice in the big man's heart, and that he'd only done the things he had under threat of the whip.

He was an innocent in all this, a victim, much like the villagers of Shafarr.

As the cries for leniency rang out within the chamber, Mu'Ungo remained impassive.

Dirk had never seen anything more dignified.

When the murmuring eventually dissipated, the Magistrate finally turned his focus to Dirk.

"And finally," the Magistrate started. "We come to you, Guildsman Vanslow."

This is it, Dirk thought.

It was the moment he'd feared since Patz had took to the witness stand…

He took a breath and steeled himself.

"I found your testimony least convincing of all."

Dirk glanced at Coen.

The young man's head was buried in his hands.

"Where your co-defendant called forward a witness to substantiate his counter-claims," he continued, "you provided no reasonable explanation to the contrary..."

Dirk dipped his head.

As expected, the Magistrate had taken Bakker's side.

"...It is therefore my opinion," he concluded, "that it was indeed you, who committed an act of murder at Shafarr and that you did so out of hatred and a desire for revenge."

Dirk shook his head in disbelief.

"Moreover," the Justice added, "by bringing this case to court, you have revealed yourself to be a liar, so in addition to the crime of murder, which this court duly bestows upon you, an additional charge of perjury will also be added to your sentence."

Things were looking bad, far worse than expected.

Right now, he'd be lucky to get twenty-five years imprisonment.

Execution seemed more likely...

Dirk's fears came true when the Justice reached beneath his desk and produced a black hat. The headwear was usually donned before a death sentence was passed.

He held his breath as the Magistrate placed it upon his head.

He turned to face Dirk.

Here it comes...

"Stop!"

The court fell silent as everyone turned towards the voice. It had come from a woman sitting in the front row of the gallery, who stood up and removed the hood from her head.

It was Marfine.

What was she doing here?

"I wish to present my evidence to the court," she declared.

The chamber erupted into a chorus of chattering, which the Justice silenced by striking the gavel with his hammer.

"The time to do that has passed," he said.

Coen leaned forward from the stalls and spoke with Vor

Ruis. The Prosecutor then raised his hand to speak.

"Yes?" the Magistrate said.

"May I approach the bench, M'Lord?"

The Justice nodded and the man came forward and proceeded to whisper something into his ear.

The Magistrate grimaced then bobbed his head.

"Very well," he said, as the Prosecutor stepped back. "The court will hear you."

Immediately, the Defence Counsel objected but his protestations were waved away.

The Clerk stood up and beckoned Marfine to the front. She took to the witness box and the Clerk approached her with a copy of the Testament.

"I will swear to the Goddess," she said.

The Clerk nodded and she made her oath.

"Please state your name for the Court," he said.

"I am Marfine Delefries," she declared. "Commander of the Elven Separatist Group, known to you as the Swords of Sheenah."

The chamber fell silent.

No one knew how to react.

The Clerk returned to his seat nervously, as Vor Ruis stood up and approached the witness box.

"You have something to say?" he asked.

"I do," she said. "I wish to speak in defence of Guildsman Vanslow."

"And what can you offer this court that we've not already heard?"

"I wish to challenge the testimony of his accuser."

The Defence Counsel stood up and raised his hand.

The Magistrate gestured for him to speak

"My client has never met this... woman," he said. "So how can she possibly refute his words?"

"Sustained," the Magistrate replied. "The witness will state for the record how she knows the Defendant."

"I don't," Marfine replied.

Her words elicited chuckles from some people in the Gallery.

She responded by cutting her eyes at them.

"…But I know the Guildsman."

"In what capacity do you know him?" the Prosecution Counsel asked.

"He was my prisoner," the She-Elf replied.

Again, the gallery fell silent.

Dirk wondered if any of them could quite believe what was going on.

"Please elaborate," the Counsel continued.

Marfine then explained in detail how her unit had captured Dirk in the gorge after Ermus and Varek had attacked him.

"So, is it fair to say," Vor interjected, "that there is no love lost between you?"

"None at all," Marfine replied.

"With this in mind, why would you choose to come here today to defend him? You must realise that in doing so, you're putting yourself at considerable risk?"

"I am aware of the consequences of my actions," she declared.

"Then why are you here?"

"To prevent a great injustice," she said.

Marfine turned her head and looked directly at the Magistrate.

"Your verdict described this man as being driven by revenge," she began. "Well, I attest that he is not."

"Why do you say this?" the Prosecutor asked.

"Because I saw it with my own eyes," she replied.

"What did you see?" Vor Ruis asked.

"The Elf who murdered Dirk's father was a rebel named Araxys," she began, "I know this because I am his daughter."

The Defence Counsel raised his hand.

"I object, M'Lord," he said. "How is any of this relevant to the case?

"Because Guildsman Vanslow was present at my father's

146

death," Marfine replied.

The Defence Counsel fell silent.

He suddenly seemed unsure how to respond.

The Prosecutor stepped forward.

"May I continue?" he asked the Magistrate.

The Justice glanced at the Defence Counsel, looking for a response, but instead he shook his head and returned to his seat.

The Magistrate gestured to the Prosecutor to proceed.

"Miss Delefries," Vor continued. "You just said that Guildsman Vanslow was present at the death of the man who killed his father?"

"Yes," she confirmed.

The Prosecutor glanced around the court.

"Well, I'm sure that I, and many people around this room, are wondering just why he was there?"

"He was trying to arrest him," Marfine said.

"Arrest him?" the Prosecutor asked.

"Yes," Marfine confirmed.

The Counsel stepped back.

"Yet despite this, your father ended up dead?"

"Yes."

Dirk glanced at the Defence Counsel, who was stifling a chuckle.

It was understandable.

Vor seemed to be leading the witness in his favour.

"This Court has heard testimonies that paint Guildsman Vanslow as a cold-blooded killer who is driven by a desire for revenge," he continued, turning to face the Gallery. "Is it not reasonable for anyone here to assume that if Guildsman Vanslow did indeed meet his father's killer – the very object of his vengeance – his first thoughts would not be to *arrest* the man, but to *kill* him?"

"Yes," Marfine responded. "If that was true... But it's not what I saw."

The Prosecutor feigned a laugh.

"So how, exactly..." he sneered, "...Did this man end up

dead, if not by the hand of his arrestor?"

"Because he was killed by someone else," she answered.

"Who?"

Marfine looked the Prosecutor in the eyes.

"Me."

The Gallery erupted into a cacophony of noise.

No one could believe quite what they had heard.

After calling for silence in the chamber, the Magistrate turned to face the She-Elf.

"Do you understand what you are doing by entering this as your testimony?" he asked.

"Like I said," she replied. "I'm here to prevent a great injustice."

"So be it," the Magistrate declared. "On the basis of your testimony, I hereby rescind the verdict levelled against Guildsman Vanslow and now find him innocent of all charges."

A chorus of cheers filled the room.

Dirk felt his heart pounding in his chest.

In a single instant, he'd gone from the depths of despair to the heights of elation.

Marfine had saved him.

But at what cost...?

He watched as the Magistrate turned to her.

"As for you, Miss Delefries," he began, "Your admission here today cannot be ignored. For the crime of murder, to which you freely confessed, I find you Guilty, and as a result, sentence you to death by hanging."

Marfine's face remained stoic.

She must have known what would happen to her all along.

Dirk knew she was principled, that she was a woman of honour and courage, but he couldn't quite fathom why she would sacrifice herself like this?

Suddenly, she drew aside her cloak and it all became clear...

Reaching down into the folds of the cloth, she produced a dagger.

The people in the gallery had barely enough time to scream as she flipped the blade in her palm then hurled it through the air toward the dock....

And buried itself in Bakker's chest.

The man gasped and reached for the blade, but he couldn't lift up his hands as his wrists were bound to the rail.

He coughed and spluttered, blood pouring from his mouth

The court ushers rushed to his aid.

But they were too late...

The dagger's edge had pierced the Guildsergeant's heart, and there was nothing they could do to save him.

As he crumpled to the floor, his hands still bound to the rail, he looked up at Dirk and mouthed a final curse before his eyes froze in the stillness of death.

Dirk glanced back at Marfine, who smiled then vaulted over the witness stand and began running toward to the doors. A group of ushers came forward to meet her, so she crossed into the pews of the gallery, hopping across the handrails to the rear of the chamber.

"Stop her!" the Magistrate yelled.

But Marfine was too quick and too nimble, and by the time the ushers had started working their way through the pews, she'd reached the far wall, where she began scaling the oaken panels to a window behind the seats.

"Don't move!" one of the men ordered.

But she was oblivious to everything but her escape.

Climbing up to the fenestra, she struck the pane with the edge of her wrist. The glass shattered and the people sitting in the seats below scurried away in fear.

The guards then began closing in on her from all sides, but as the nearest one reached out to seize her ankle, she quickly pulled it away and disappeared through the window.

The Magistrate was furious.

He seemed incensed that someone would be so brazen as to defile his courtroom, and started striking his hammer indiscriminately across his desk, the sides of his mouth frothing white with rage.

Outside, Dirk heard the whinnying of a horse then the sound of hooves thundering over cobbles.

She had escaped.

CHAPTER 17

"What'll you do now?" Coen asked, as he accompanied Dirk down the Courthouse steps.

"I'll return to the Guild..." he replied. "...Continue my service."

The blonde-haired Guildsman laughed.

"I'd have thought you'd want a holiday after everything you've been through?"

"I do," he replied. "That's why I'm asking for a posting in Durnborg. Ing said it was quiet up there, a good place to pass the time..."

Coen shook his head and smiled.

"I thought you didn't like being bored," he said.

Dirk laughed.

"I think I've had more than my fair share of excitement recently..."

They continued to the bottom, where a large crowd had gathered at the foot of the steps. Many were simply well-wishers, but some of them wore press pins and were carrying quills and scrolls.

As he approached them, they barraged him with a series of questions.

"How does it feel to be vindicated?"

"Are you happy with the verdict?"

"Will you be returning to Ghis?"

He ignored them all

In amongst the throng, he noticed a man wearing a tunic that was embroidered with the Emperor's motif.

"You," Dirk said. "Are you with the Imperial Post?"

"Yes," the man replied.

"Good," Dirk replied. "Write this down."

The man held up his pen as Dirk began to dictate.

"For too long," he began, "the Empire has ignored the plight of the Elves in Gefghed. The city of Ghis is overflowing with the poor and the desperate. It's no wonder they've turned to crime. I hope my trial serves to highlight what's happening south of the border so that proper action can be taken to enforce the law and end injustice in the colonies."

The scribe gave him a cursory look.

"That's all very well," he said, "But what our readers really want to know is whether you feel justice has been served?"

Out of the corner of his eye, Dirk saw Mu'Ungo being led away by a group of ushers. His hands and feet were chained, and they were shunting him towards an armoured prison wagon that had been parked on the street.

"I don't feel any calmer," he replied morosely.

The man scribed the words on his scroll.

"And what are your thoughts on the She-Elf?" he asked. "Are you glad she did what she did?"

His answer was 'yes' before he could open his lips Coen stepped forward and put his arm between them.

"We'll answer all your questions later," he said. "My friend has been through a lot and needs to rest."

They picked their way through the crowd and began making their way down the street.

"Thanks for saving me," Dirk said.

"It's what friends are for," Coen chuckled.

As they passed the adjoining alleyway Dirk saw a group of Guardsmen gathered beneath the broken window, where Marfine had made her escape.

"Do you know what happened to her?" he asked.

"As far as we know, she fled town and was last seen heading south."

Dirk allowed himself a wry smile.

He was glad she'd made it.

If not for her, he'd be on the prison wagon with Mu'Ungo, heading south.

He wondered to himself why she'd gone so far out of her way to save him?

Maybe she hadn't?

Maybe the whole thing had been part of her plan to get to Bakker?

But if that was the case, why bother even taking the stand? Given her skills with a dagger, she could have easily thrown it at him from the stalls or the gallery.

It bothered him not knowing, and he would have liked to ask her why.

It all seemed odd.

There was another thing too...

Her testimony had originally been declined.

Had it not been for Coen's intervention, she'd have not stood in the witness box at all.

"So, what did you say to him?" Dirk asked.

"To whom?" Coen replied.

"Vor," Dirk said. "You whispered something to him, before he spoke to the Magistrate."

Coen smiled.

"You really want to know?" he replied.

"What you said saved my life," Dirk said.

His friend laughed.

"I told him to tell Arneld that he was being investigated for corruption, and it would not help his case if he was seen to be impeding witnesses."

Dirk was confused.

"Arneld was on the take?" he said. "I thought you said he was a good man?"

"I did," Coen replied glibly. "Who would have known, eh?"

"So, you lied?"

Coen smirked.

"He didn't know that."

Dirk shook his head.

The revelation shocked him.

It was hard to believe a Magistrate could be corrupted, and not least one that worked for the Guild...

"Are all Judges corrupt?" Dirk asked.

Coen puffed out his cheeks.

"Corruption is everywhere..." he replied "...And in places you wouldn't expect."

Dirk reflected on his words as they made their way to the Guildhouse, wondering if he would encounter anything similar in Durnborg?

It was a much smaller town, which implied much smaller problems. The worst he was likely to encounter would be Guildsmen stealing extra croissants from the mess...

Then again, *who knew?*

APPENDICES

Geography

Ethren – A Realm of Kingdoms located to the North West of the Great Continent, consisting of the Gerwaldian Empire and the Kingdoms of Westren. The common language is *Prutch*.

Western Ocean – A large ocean lying off the western cost of Westren.

Middle Sea – A small sea that separates Grexia from the continent of Kulaani.

Gerwald – Kingdom in Eastern Ethren
    Royal Kronnig – Capital City of the Empire of Gerwald, located centrally on the River Rhund.
    Hellenburg – A City in central Gerwald.
    Einhof – A town in eastern Gerwald, headquarters of the Guild Corps.
    Durnborg – A small town in northern Gerwald.
    Neinborn – A town in the Eastern Kingdom on Ethren, site of a famous battle.
    Rhund – A town in Gerwald.
    The River Rhund – A major waterway that flows from the Grondils through the Gerwaldian Empire and Gefghed to the Middle Sea.

Westren – The collective name for the Kingdoms of Hussfalt, Hessell, La Broque and Grexia.

Hessell – Western Ethren Kingdom, located south of the River Soude and north of the River Slou, bordered by the Grondil Mountains to the East.

> **Wernerliecht** – Capital of Hessell, which sits at the mouth of the River Slou.
>
> **Eindbosch** – A town in southeast Hessell, sitting in the foothills of the Grondil Range.
>
> **The Rivertowns** – Collective name for Grente, Grice and Utterdam: the three major towns that are situated on the River Soude.
>
> **Grente** – Port city to the North West of Hessell. Famous for its bridge, named after the Hessellian Prince Wendell, and University.
>
> **Grente Quarry** – A prison and quarry that is famous for its sandstone.
>
> **Leiderbrugge** – a small town within the county of Grente.
>
> **Woergeld** – a small town within the county of Grente.
>
> **Utterdam** – A city on the banks of the Soude, lying East of the town of Grice. Houses the Guildschool of Hessell and Utterdam Sanctuary.
>
> **Grice** – A town on the banks of the Soude, lying to the West of Utterdam.
>
> **Delstad** – A small village in Western Hessell, most famous for the Delstad Estate, a vast stately built upon the coastal cliffs.

> **The River Slou** – A border river that divides the Kingdoms of Hessell and La Broque
>
> **The Soude** – A border river that divides the kingdoms of Hessell and Hussfalt.
>
> > **The Northern Byway** – The main road connecting the three Rivertowns.

Grondil – A mountainous region in the northwest of Hessell, also the source of the River Soude.

    Siegmur's Pass – A pass in the Grondil range that links the Kingdoms of Hussfalt and Hessell, now closed following a rock fall.

    Baan – A large village in the Grondil foothills, famous for its timber products.

Hussfalt – A Westren Kingdom, located to the immediate north of the River Soude

    Busque – Capital City of Hussfalt.

    Marnberg – a small village that sits near the Striffen Line.

    Bladenhaal – A village in Hussfalt, the site of a famous battle.

    Kronnick – A town in Hussfalt, site of a famous battle during the Great Westren War.

    Wemmelford – A village in Hussfalt.

    Deneul – River in southern Hussfalt.

    Thishen – A village in eastern Hussfalt.

    Striffen Line - A heavily fortified range of hills roughly five miles to the north of Grice.

La Broque – A Westren Kingdom located to the South of Hessell.

    Slou – A river in that marks the border between La Broque and Hessell.

    Pendforte – a city in the Kingdom of La Broque, South West of Ethren.

    Basteaux – A village in the Kingdom of La Broque, South West of Ethren.

Grexia – Kingdom in South Westren, said to be the oldest Kingdom in Ethren.

    Corinthe – Capital of Grexia.

        Summer Festival – An annual event featuring the

best travelling circuses in all of Ethren.

Temple of the Saints – A famous cathedral, and permanent residence of the Grand Alterman, spiritual leader of the V'Loirean faith.

Doran – A small village in eastern Grexia that sits on the coast of the Middle Sea.

Nysos – A port town in eastern Grexia that sits on the coast of the Middle Sea.

Daxus – An island city-state, aligned to the Kingdom of Grexia.

Harardren – A Kingdom in the Northern Realms. It is located North of Hussfalt, beyond the River Vardeaen and is chiefly populated by Dwarfs.

River Vardeaen – River that separates Westren from the Northern Realms.

Bim-Lodhar – Capital of Harardren.

Heg-Logar - City located in Harardren, famous for the *Grey Kirk*, a famous V'Loirean Cathedral.

Kulaani – A Realm of Kingdoms located to the south of the Gerwaldian colonies of Tibrut and Marmur.

B'Naatu – A city in Kulaani, south of the Gerwaldian colonies of Tibrut and Marmur.

Gefghed – A kingdom located to the south east of Ethren, currently under the rule of the Gerwaldian Empire. It is sometimes known as *Shemali*.

Ghis – Capital of Gefghed, located in the West of the Kingdom, at the mouth of the River Rhund.

Shemali – A small town on the River Rhund.

Shafarr – A small village lying on the edge of Shula's Gorge.

Shida – A small village in Gefghed and rumoured birthplace of the prophet V'Loire.

The Silent Valley – A dry canyon that marks the border between Gerwald and Gefghed.

Veleenum – The last Kingdom of the Elves, located to the East of Gerwald in the Zamur Mountains.

Characters

Guildsmen

Dirk Vanslow – A Guildsman.

Guildmaster Patrick – Head of the Gerwaldian Guild-school in Royal Kronnig.

Major Patz – Master of Arms at the Gerwaldian Guild-school in Royal Kronnig.

Coen – A Guildsman.

Ing – A Guildsman.

Guildsergeant Bakker – Leader of the Red Vipers of Ghis.

Varek – A Guildsman serving with the Red Vipers.

Mu'Ungo – A Kulaanian Guildsman serving with the Red Vipers.

Ermus – A Guildsman serving with the Red Vipers.

Kort – A Grexian Guildsman serving with the Red Vipers.

Boors – A Half-Dwarf Guildsman serving with the Red Vipers.

Citizens of Ghis

Minas Vanslow – Father of Dirk Vanslow.

Ruyven – a former Rebel, now owner of Ruyven's Rums.

Rebels

Araxys Delefries - Rebel leader of the Swords of Sheenah.

Marfine Delefries - A rebel, serving with Swords of Sheenah, daughter of Araxys.

Olojeon Hax – A rebel, serving with Swords of Sheenah.

Tressyn – A rebel, serving with Swords of Sheenah.

Dustyn – A rebel, serving with Swords of Sheenah.

Einhof

Justice Arneld – A Magistrate

Vor Ruis – A young lawyer

Royal Kronnig

Bartheld – Innkeep and owner of the Emperor's Legs.

Religion

V'Loire – God-Prophet and founder of the V'Loirean Faith.

> The Testament – The holy book of the V'Loirean Faith
>
> St. Felix – One of V'Loire's nine disciples, known as *The Beastmaster* or *Master of Beasts*.
>
> St. Greta – One of V'Loire's nine disciples, known as the *Prophet of Doom*, as it was said she could foresee the future.
>
> St. Unglebus – One of V'Loire's nine disciples, a patron of the arts, who came to be known as *The Drinker*.

Sheenah – God-Prophet and founder of the Sheenahic Faith.

> The She'En – The holy book of the Sheenahic Faith.

Tekat – A god of death, whose worshippers make human sacrifices. Also known as the *Horned God* or the *Horned Devil*.

Printed in Great Britain
by Amazon